## DANGER ON THE TRAIL!

Carole was enjoying her trail ride with Scott and the other tourists when the sky suddenly brightened with a distant flash of lightning. Carole frowned, knowing there would be trouble.

The problem was that Scott's mount, Patch, was frightened by thunder or anything that sounded like it. His reaction was to bolt and there was no way a non-rider like Scott could handle it.

The whole world went into slow motion for the few seconds it took Carole to dash over to Patch. As she neared the horse she could see that his ears were laid flat back on his head, and the whites of his eyes showed his terror.

There wouldn't be time for Scott to dismount and Carole to mount before the rumble of thunder began. Without even thinking about it, Carole used a rock as a launchpad and leapt up onto Patch, behind Scott. But before she could grab the reins from his hand, the roll of thunder began. Then there was another brilliant streak of lightning nearer by and the roaring crack of thunder.

Patch took off!

Bantam Books in THE SADDLE CLUB series. Ask your bookseller for the books you have missed:

# THE SADDLE CLUB

# TRAIL MATES

## BONNIE BRYANT

A BANTAM BOOK®

NEW YORK · TORONTO · LONDON · SYDNEY · AUCKLAND

# THE SADDLE CLUB: TRAIL MATES
## A BANTAM BOOK 0 553 40012 6

First published in USA by Bantam Skylark Books.
First publication in Great Britain

PRINTING HISTORY
Bantam edition published 1989
Reprinted 1990, 1992, 1993

Bantam Books are published by Transworld Publishers
Ltd., 61–63 Uxbridge Road, Ealing, London W5 5SA, in
Australia by Transworld Publishers (Australia) Pty. Ltd.,
15–25 Helles Avenue, Moorebank, NSW 2170, and in New
Zealand by Transworld Publishers (N.Z.) Ltd., 3 William
Pickering Drive, Albany, Auckland.

Printed and bound in Great Britain by
Cox & Wyman Ltd., Reading, Berks.

For my trail mates,
Neil, Emmons, & Andrew

CAROLE HANSON STEAMED up the walkway and through the door into Pine Hollow Stables. Her wavy black hair bounced against her shoulders with each step. She hated being late to anything, especially to riding classes. She stomped into the locker room and tossed her knapsack angrily on the floor.

"What's gotten into you?" asked Stevie Lake, one of her two best friends.

Carole grimaced. She really didn't feel like giving a long explanation about how her father's friend Lynne Blessing had insisted on driving her to the stables— and on making her late. "Somebody gave me a lift," she said. "And I would have been better off on the bus."

"Oh," Stevie said, pulling on her boots. "Well, if

you're already in a good mood, you'll be glad to know that we're going to be working on changing gaits in class today."

"Groan," Carole remarked.

"What's the matter with working on changing gaits?" Lisa Atwood asked. Along with Stevie and Carole, Lisa made up the trio that called themselves The Saddle Club. The girls were devoted to horses—and to each other. Although Lisa was the oldest of the three, she had the least experience as a rider, having begun only a few months earlier. Max Regnery, their riding teacher and the owner of Pine Hollow Stables, felt that Lisa had a lot of promise, but she also had a lot to learn.

"There's nothing wrong with changing gaits," Carole explained. "Changing gaits is very important. But it's something I can do pretty well already. I was hoping we'd work on something a little more challenging in class this morning. At least then I would have rushed for a reason!" She smiled ever so slightly. Her anger at Lynne was wearing off. It was always hard for Carole to remain angry for long, especially when she was within a few feet of a horse.

"Maybe there *will* be a challenge this morning," Stevie said temptingly. She stood up and selected one of the velvet-covered hard hats from a hook on the wall where they were stored. Standing in front of the mirror, she slipped it on her head and snapped the chin strap tightly. Lisa and Carole took hats as well. Carole didn't bother to look at herself in the mirror while she snapped the strap. She knew that the hats looked weird and that adjusting them in the mirror wouldn't make the slightest bit of difference. But they were required for safety, and even the newest rider knew it was a good idea to protect herself against a possible fall.

"Okay, I give up," Carole said after a moment. "What makes you think there might be a challenge today?"

Stevie's eyes twinkled. She was a teaser and a practical joker. She loved it that she'd piqued Carole's curiosity. "It may be nothing," she began, "but Max was here a while ago. He was looking for you—"

"Me?" Carole interrupted.

"—*and* me," Stevie added. "Said he'd talk to us together when you got here. Ready?" she asked.

In spite of herself, Carole glanced at the mirror. Satisfied with what she saw, she nodded at Stevie. "Come on, Lisa," she said. "Maybe it'll be a challenge for you, too."

"Changing gaits is a challenge for me," Lisa reminded her friends, but she fell in line behind the other girls. They headed toward the stable area, where the other students were already doing their chores.

As the girls entered the long hallway by the box

3

stalls, they spotted Max standing next to the largest stall at the end of the row. It housed Delilah, a palomino mare, and her young colt, Samson. Max appeared to be watching Samson, but Carole knew that he was actually overseeing all the chores his students were doing.

"Polly!" he called out to one of the girls. "You must not yank the straps when you're tightening the girth. All you'll get for your troubles is a kick!" Polly looked up guiltily from the left side of her horse. She hadn't known Max was watching.

"Just wait until he breathes out, then you can tighten it easily," Max advised.

"He's holding his breath, Max," Polly complained.

"But he can't hold it forever," Max reminded her.

Carole stifled a smile. She knew that there was an awful lot to learn about taking care of horses, but much of it was just plain common sense. Polly would learn these things in time.

"Well, good morning, Carole," Max greeted her. "Glad you could join us today."

"I'm sorry, but I couldn't help being late," Carole began the explanation of her exasperating morning. "This friend of my dad's wanted to give me a ride, but she kept talking to Dad; I *knew* we'd be late, but she wouldn't stop, so—" Carole stopped talking. She could see that Max didn't really care why she was late.

He just wanted her to know that he had noticed. Max could be very relaxed about some things, but not when it came to the stable and riding horses. He was very strict about training discipline, and that included promptness.

"I wanted to ask you or Stevie to help me out with something."

One of the traditions at Pine Hollow, which was located in Willow Creek, Virginia, not far from Washington, D.C., was that all of the students helped with the routine chores. Not only did that help keep their costs down, but it gave the students chances to learn more about horse care. Since Carole's ambition was to spend the rest of her life with horses—riding, raising, or training them—she was always interested in new opportunities.

"I have a group of tourists who want to take a trail ride. There are about ten riders. Red O'Malley can lead the group, but I don't know how well trained any of them are. I'd like to know there's another experienced rider with them. Would either of you be willing to cut class to go out with Red and this group?"

Riding with a group of tourists was not exactly Carole's idea of a challenge. She looked at Stevie. Stevie's eyes rolled up to the ceiling. It was clear that she wasn't too enthusiastic about it either. On the other hand, Carole thought to herself, it might be good experience. After all, if she was going to be an instructor someday, she'd be working with lots of new riders.

She shrugged. "Sure, Max, I'll do it," she volunteered.

"Thanks, Carole. Go find Red. You and he can choose the horses for the group. I told Red to take the hill trail and then come back through Brown's farm. The tourists will love the pasture. Don't let them stop by the creek, though. They'll have the horses drinking no matter what, and then . . ."

Carole listened carefully as Max gave his instructions. She realized that she had been right to agree to this assignment. There *was* a lot to learn. When Max finally finished, she saluted him smartly, just the way she had seen her father, a Marine Corps colonel, do. Then she clicked her heels together for good measure and marched off to find Red.

"See you in class, Max," Stevie said, turning to go back to the tack room.

"Not so fast," Max said, halting her. "There are still fifteen minutes before your class," he reminded her. "Don't you have a chore to do?"

From Max, those could be very significant words. Stevie knew that if she didn't come up with something quickly, she was likely to find herself pitchforking straw. She'd rather go on a trail ride with *fifty* tourists than that. Lisa came to her rescue.

"We were right in the middle of soaping the dressage saddles, Max," she said.

"Right in the middle?" he asked suspiciously.

Stevie and Lisa nodded in unison.

"Then I guess you'd better finish before class," he said, smiling at them. "I'll get somebody else to keep an eye on Samson when we let him out in the paddock by himself."

"Oh, no," Lisa groaned, giving herself away.

"But I know how eager you must be to finish the dressage saddles, so off with you. And if you want to cut class to finish the job . . ."

His voice trailed off. Stevie and Lisa definitely did *not* want to take him up on that suggestion!

Lisa and Stevie returned to the tack room. Each removed a dressage saddle from storage and placed it on a rack for cleaning. They talked as they worked, Stevie trying to give Lisa pointers on changing gaits.

". . . So, when you want to slow down, say from trot to walk, you really kind of sit *into* the saddle, leaning back a little."

"And pull on the reins?" Lisa asked.

"Sure, a bit, but you do more of the work with your *seat* than with your hands. And you never yank on the reins."

"I know that," Lisa said. "Everybody knows that."

"Not everybody," Stevie said significantly. She tilted

7

her head over toward the locker area of the tack room. There, primping in front of the dingy mirror, was Veronica diAngelo.

Veronica was the only daughter of a very wealthy and influential family and she never let anybody to forget it. She always dressed perfectly in the most expensive clothes. Her mother drove a Mercedes. So did her father. They had even bought Veronica an extremely valuable Thoroughbred stallion named Cobalt. But money couldn't buy everything, and one of the things it hadn't bought Veronica was responsibility. Because of Veronica's ignorance and carelessness, Cobalt had had a fatal accident.

Now, while Stevie and Lisa watched, Veronica combed her hair so that every inch of it shone. She carefully applied lip gloss and pinched her cheeks to make them pink. She straightened her collar and smoothed her riding jacket, checking to be sure the pocket flaps lay flat along the perfectly matched pattern of the expensive fabric.

"Are you going to a movie set or a riding ring?" Stevie asked. Stevie was not very good at keeping her opinions to herself. Lisa stifled a laugh. Veronica arched her eyebrows.

"It may interest you to know that I'll probably be doing some of both today, in a manner of speaking."

"In a manner of speaking?" Stevie echoed. *Nobody* talked that way.

"In case you didn't know, there is a photographer here at the stable today. She's a local woman, but she's trying to make it into the high-fashion photography world. She's looking for promising young riders to model for her. She's currently doing work for a catalog. Naturally, she'll want the best-dressed and best-looking girls to use for the catalog. Although it's not much of a start, it *is* a start. I think I'll enjoy it. And then, of course, there's the money . . ."

Finally satisfied with her own reflection, Veronica nodded farewell to Stevie and Lisa and drifted out of the tack room. She was carrying her hard hat. She always put it on at the last possible moment so it wouldn't ruin her hairdo.

"Grrr," Stevie remarked when Veronica had left the tack room. "That girl is the most annoying, obnoxious, yucky person I have ever known."

"I didn't know you liked her that much," Lisa joked.

"I don't," Stevie said, laughing at Lisa's joke. "I was just being nice. But you know who I feel sorry for? I feel sorry for the poor photographer who ends up with her as a model. I bet she'll be even worse to work with as a model than she is as a rider."

Lisa nodded. Anything that would inflate Veronica's

oversize ego would make her worse. Modeling would certainly do that.

Just then, the P.A. scratched to life. "Flat class will begin in three minutes," Max announced.

"And we still have to tack up our horses!" Lisa yowled. "Let's go!"

THE TRAIL RIDERS were part of a group of tourists staying near Pine Hollow. None of them was an experienced rider.

"Now put your left foot in the stirrup and lift yourself up," Carole instructed one of the trail riders, Dr. Babcock. "Be careful you don't jump and land too hard on the horse's . . ."

She stopped talking because the man wasn't listening to her. He nearly flew into the air and plopped himself down in the saddle. His horse grunted. Carole patted the horse sympathetically and helped Dr. Babcock adjust his stirrups.

He was the second-to-last rider she had to help mount before they could begin the trail ride. His son, Scott, was her final task. When Dr. Babcock began walking his horse over to the rest of the group, Carole turned her attention to Scott.

"Did you see what your father did?" she asked. Scott nodded. "Don't do it that way," she said. Scott grinned.

"Dad's not very good at listening to directions," he explained.

"How about you?" Carole asked.

"Try me," he said.

Carole carefully told him the steps to follow in mounting a horse. She explained that landing hard on the horse's back was a strain on the animal's spine.

"I could tell the horse didn't like it," Scott said. "So I suppose all that stuff about the cowboy jumping down from the second-story window into his saddle to make a getaway is just Hollywood junk, right?"

"Right," Carole said with a grin. Then, when Scott was in the saddle, she helped him with his stirrups and showed him how to hold the reins. When she was satisfied, she mounted her own horse, Diablo, and they joined the others for the trail ride.

It was a relaxed ride. The horses at Pine Hollow were usually used for classes, which could be quite strenuous for them. When Max had a group of inexperienced riders who wanted to ride on a trail, it meant that the horses would be walking slowly for an hour or more. Max would not let untested riders canter or even trot. Not only could the riders get into trouble, but the horses would be at risk, and Max would never let that happen.

Carole rode Diablo at the rear of the group. The riders had been paired and her trail mate was Scott Babcock. She wasn't paying too much attention to him, though. Carole's job, as second rider, was to watch ahead and be sure that nobody was getting into any trouble. Most of the riders in this group seemed so unfamiliar with horses that they weren't trying anything risky at all. She watched the riders keenly, but spared some of her attention for appreciating her surroundings.

It was a muggy, hot summer day. Threatening clouds masked the sunshine, but there was no relief from the humidity. As the group entered a forest path that led up a hillside, Carole sighed, expecting some relief. There was none. The mosquitoes and gnats were out in full force. The horses' tails swished, flicking at insects. Carole swatted a mosquito on her arm. Then, when another one landed on Diablo's neck, she swatted that as well. Diablo nodded his head ever so slightly after her hand struck. He seemed grateful, but too hot himself to react much.

"Doesn't it bother him when you hit him like that?" Scott asked.

"Not when I'm doing him a favor and he knows it,"

Carole told him. "Horses are tough. You can hurt one, that's for sure, but Diablo knows the difference between, say, a friendly swat like that and a punishing whack, which I might give him if he started to bite me or something."

"Have you been riding a long time?" Scott asked.

"Since I could walk," Carole said. "I was raised on Marine Corps bases, and there are usually stables on bases, so I got to spend a lot of time riding. I plan to own horses when I grow up. I may become a vet, too. I'm not sure about that yet."

"You seem to know an awful lot about horses already," Scott said, obviously impressed.

Carole thought about her friend Kate Devine, now living with her family on a dude ranch out west. Now *Kate* knew about horses and riding! Carole really missed the championship rider, and hoped to visit Kate soon. In fact, she'd already saved up a lot of the money she would need for airfare.

Still thinking about Kate, Carole shrugged off Scott's compliment. "This is just basic stuff," she said. "In classes, I'm working on harder things, like jumping and dressage."

"Dressage? You mean like putting costumes on the horses?"

Carole couldn't help it. She burst into giggles. "No. Dressage is an important aspect of riding, especially in competition. It focuses on the horse's training, but it's the rider's responsibility to see that the horse does what he's supposed to do. It has to do with obedience and manners."

"Really? How do you teach a horse manners?"

Almost before she knew what she was doing, Carole was off and talking. Carole's good friends knew that she could talk about horses for hours. Stevie and Lisa teased her about it sometimes, reminding Carole that they already had one teacher, Max, and didn't really need another. But Scott had never heard this before. When he appeared interested, it was all the encouragement she needed.

After about ten minutes of her lecture, Carole brought herself to an abrupt halt. "I can't believe I'm doing this," she told Scott. "I just start talking about horses, and there's no stopping me. I'm sorry."

"No, don't be sorry," Scott protested, smiling at her. "It's really interesting. I mean, as much as I can *understand* is really interesting. How did you learn all this?"

"Just by caring," she said. "And speaking of caring, I'm going to have to pay a little more attention to the other riders. Excuse me."

With that, Carole nudged Diablo into a faster pace so she could catch up with Dr. Babcock, who was having some trouble. He was a few riders in front of them, but his horse was lagging behind. Dr. Babcock was trying to get the animal to go faster by kicking at him. The horse was ignoring the kicks.

"Chip is stubborn, Dr. Babcock," she explained, drawing up to him. "He likes things just so and gets a kick out of ignoring riders. I think he's been annoyed with you since you landed so hard on his back. You need to show him who's the boss, though, or he'll just get more and more stubborn."

"Isn't that dangerous?"

"No, because Chip's idea of how to be stubborn is to walk slowly and that's not dangerous. He needs to pick up his pace, but he doesn't like to be kicked. When he gets so poky, you should use your calf to put pressure on his belly. First your right leg, then your left, alternating with each step. Now, try it."

This time, Dr. Babcock tried to follow Carole's instructions, and it worked. Soon Chip and Dr. Babcock were catching up with the other riders. Carole dropped back to the rear, behind Scott, who was riding Patch.

"Nice work," Scott said, admiring Carole's success with his father.

"It's nothing," Carole said. "That's easy stuff."

"Well, then, I guess I'd like to see you doing some of the hard stuff," he told her.

Carole just nodded in acknowledgment. It felt a little odd to have Scott ask so many questions and admire her skills so frankly. He didn't seem *that* interested in riding himself. He just wanted to know about her. Carole had just started to think about what that might mean when her thoughts were suddenly turned elsewhere.

The clouds, which had been blanketing the sun all morning, now darkened menacingly. She didn't like the idea of having all these tourists out in the woods if it began raining, but that would be nothing compared to what might happen if there were thunder and lightning, especially thunder. When the sky suddenly brightened with a distant flash of lightning, Red O'Malley brought the group to a halt and turned toward the back of the line of riders. Carole knew that she and Red had the same thought at the same instant.

The problem was that Patch, normally a very docile horse, was frightened by thunder, or anything that sounded like it. His reaction was to bolt and there was no way a nonrider like Scott could manage it.

"Carole, get on Patch!" Red cried because he wouldn't be able to reach Patch in time to calm him himself.

Without hesitating, Carole dismounted from Diablo and half-hitched him to a branch. "Hold the reins tight," she called to Scott, running. "I'll be right there!"

Scott looked at her quizzically. There was no time to explain to him. She just had to hope he would listen.

The whole world went into slow motion for the few

seconds it took Carole to dash over to Patch. As she neared the horse she could see that his ears were laid flat back on his head, and the whites of his eyes showed his terror. Patch had seen the lightning and knew what was coming.

There wouldn't be time for Scott to dismount and Carole could mount before the rumble of thunder began. Without even thinking about it, Carole used a rock as a launchpad, and leapt up onto Patch, behind Scott. She reached around the astonished boy, but before she could grab the reins from his hand, the roll of thunder began. Then there was another brilliant streak of lightning nearer by and the roaring crack of thunder.

Patch took off!

Carole knew there was a big difference between the controlled gait of a properly behaved horse and the frantic gallop of one that was terrified. Patch raced into the woods without any thought of his own safety or that of his riders. Branches whipped at Carole and Scott from both sides. They were off the trail and their legs were battered by the bushes. One of Scott's feet was torn from its stirrup by the bushes as they passed.

Carole wrested the reins from Scott's frozen grasp and tried to maintain enough balance from where she sat on Patch's rump to control the terrified animal. She leaned to the right so she could see where they were headed, but when she saw it she didn't like it at all. They were aimed directly at a low-slung branch.

"Duck!" she cried, pushing Scott forward next to Patch's mane on the left side. She could see the boy's white knuckles grasping the thick hair of the horse's mane. The horse was totally out of control as they raced under the low-slung branch that scraped Carole's back. At least she was still on the horse.

Finally Carole managed to grip the reins properly in her hands. Then she began to tighten up on them slowly. She knew that eventually Patch would tire and stop running, but until then she was responsible for Scott's safety as well as her own. She needed to minimize the damage. And the damage could be considerable. Patch began plunging down a hill so fast that his front feet had trouble keeping up with his rear feet. If that continued for long, he'd be in danger of falling down.

"Grip tight with your legs," Carole gasped.

"I can't," Scott said, fear evident in his voice. "I lost one stirrup and my foot slipped through the other one. It's around my ankle!"

That was worse than losing the stirrup, Carole knew. It meant that if Scott *did* lose his balance, he'd be dragged by the horse!

Patch zigzagged downhill, along an old trail. Carole realized, with a sick feeling, that the trail had been abandoned after a hurricane had knocked down some very big trees across it. And there was one of them, right up ahead!

Carole shortened the reins even more but Patch didn't break stride. He galloped up to the decaying pine tree and then rose into the air, high above it. Carole felt Scott begin to lose his grip, sliding to the left. With every ounce of strength she had, she held him tight, counterbalancing him. She knew that if they weren't balanced when Patch landed, it would be all over.

When the horse's feet struck the ground, Carole and Scott managed to stay on. Carole gripped the horse tightly with her legs. Then, as suddenly as he had started, Patch stopped. He pulled to a halt, sniffed the air, blew out briskly, and began nibbling on some weeds that grew by the side of the path.

"Have we landed?" Scott asked, his voice shaking.

"Looks that way," Carole told him, slipping down off Patch's back. "You want to get down?"

Scott nodded numbly. Carole helped him remove his foot from the stirrup and explained how to dismount. Following her instructions, he slid down the side of Patch's saddle. When he was safely on the ground, he reached for the trunk of a nearby tree for support. He was shaking all over.

Carole turned her attention to Patch. Other than

being sweaty from his gallop on a muggy day, he was unharmed and now seemed uninterested in the gentle rumble of thunder they could hear in the distance. She took the horse's reins and tugged at them gently to get his attention.

"Come on, Scott, we'd better get back to the group. They'll be worried about us, you know." She turned Patch to face the slope where she knew they would find Red and the other riders.

Scott stood up straight, wiped his hand across his forehead, and joined Carole.

"You saved my life, you know," he said as they walked along.

"Oh, I don't think there was *that* much danger," she said, shrugging, not wanting to think about the stinging she felt from the branches that had just grazed her arms, legs, and back.

"No, I mean it, Carole. You saved my life," Scott said again. "You're *something*!"

Carole sighed to herself. After all, she hadn't done anything that any other experienced rider wouldn't have done, and that was why she'd been on the trail ride in the first place.

"That's what trail mates are for," she said.

"NOW, TROT!" MAX called out to his students, who were cantering in a large circle around the outdoor ring.

Lisa shifted her weight, sitting down into the saddle and straightening her back. Pepper, her black-speckled gray horse, kept on cantering. She made a determined face and gripped harder with her calves, shortening the reins. She needed to show Pepper who was in charge. He slowed down to a trot.

"Lisa, you must have better control," Max reminded her. "You should be able to change gaits within two paces. Three at the most. Now watch his trot. Pepper wants to walk—see how he's slowing down. Keep your leg on him! Use the whip!"

Lisa tried to follow all of Max's instructions. It wasn't easy, but with some effort she found that Pepper had a nice even trot and she was rising and sitting with it in a proper post.

"Better," Max said. From Max, that was high praise.

Lisa continued to concentrate very hard on her gaits and changing them. She was only vaguely aware of the click-whir of a camera nearby. She realized that those sounds must be coming from the photographer Veronica had mentioned. Lisa glanced across the ring for a second. What she saw made her giggle.

The photographer was perched on top of the wooden fence that surrounded the ring. And in front of her was Veronica, prancing back and forth on her horse. The girl was trying to look casual, but the effect was anything but casual. She flipped her long black hair back over her shoulder and tossed her head. Then she removed her riding hat to show off her hair. Veronica was letting her horse get in everybody else's way so she could do most of her work right in front of the photographer. But the woman seemed oblivious to Veronica's obvious moves. The camera kept clicking.

"Five minutes remaining," Max announced. "That means you too, Veronica," he said pointedly. "We will walk our horses to cool them down, starting . . . now!"

Quickly, Lisa got Pepper to switch from a trot to a

walk. She was pretty sure she'd even managed it within two paces and was about to congratulate herself when she noticed it had begun to rain.

"Okay, so we'll walk them around the indoor ring," Max told his students. They dismounted and led their horses through the stable area to the indoor ring.

Stevie led her horse, Comanche, next to Lisa and Pepper.

"Did you notice the high-fashion model?" Stevie asked, making a gagging motion.

"Who could miss her?" Lisa agreed, giggling. "My favorite part was when she took off her hat and shook her hair loose. Who does she think she is, anyway?"

"She thinks she's Veronica diAngelo—and that's good enough for *her*," Stevie said. "The only trouble is that she thinks it ought to be good enough for everybody else, too!"

Stevie heard the now-familiar click of the photographer's camera and felt Comanche tense up. His ears went flat against his head. Stevie knew he was upset. Quickly, she shortened her grip on the reins, and then patted him reassuringly on his neck.

"There, there, boy," she said. "Don't be afraid. It's just a camera, and you can be sure that Veronica is somewhere between you and it!"

Comanche relaxed.

"Veronica?" a woman's voice said. Stevie and Lisa

turned to see the photographer standing behind them. "Is she the black-haired girl who kept getting in my way during class?" she asked.

Lisa nodded. Stevie started laughing. "I don't think that's what *she'd* call it, though," she said.

"There's always one," the woman said. Then she extended her hand. "My name's Jacqueline Small. Call me Jackie."

The girls introduced themselves and shook hands.

"Did you enjoy the class?" Stevie asked her.

"I learned a lot," Jackie said. "A lot. Thanks for letting me sit in."

"No problem," Stevie told her. "Come back anytime."

"Oh, I will," Jackie said. "See you!" With that, she closed her camera case and left the stable.

Lisa watched Jackie as she walked quickly toward the stable door. "Nice lady," she said, thinking out loud. Then Pepper tugged at the reins. He was eager to return to his stall and have a drink of water. "I know, I know," she said. "Come on, it's lunchtime."

"Yeah, it *is*," Stevie said, leading Comanche into his stall. "And where's our trail boss, Carole? Think she got lost?"

"NOW, DON'T LET your horses start going too fast just because we're close to home," Carole warned the riders near her. "It's not good for them to run at the end of a ride, and it's a bad habit to let them get into," she explained.

Scott was once again riding on Patch. It had taken all of Carole's persuasive powers to get him to mount Patch again, but, in the end, he'd done it.

"Is there anything about riding you don't know?" Scott asked.

The questioned annoyed Carole. Of course there were things she didn't know about riding and about horses—lots of them. It was just that *he* knew so little.

"Yes," she told him. "I don't know how to stand on a horse's bare back and skip rope."

"I saw somebody do that in a circus once," Scott said. Her sarcasm had been lost on him and she was a little ashamed of herself for having said what she did.

"I was just teasing," she explained. "But there *are* a lot of things I don't know about horses. These animals are a lifetime of work and learning. You can learn enough to be comfortable with them in just a few years, but to learn everything? Well, nobody knows everything."

Scott looked like he wanted to say something, but he sighed instead. Carole was relieved. The situation made her uncomfortable. She was glad when the line of riders finally entered the yard next to the stable and it was time to dismount. She would be too busy with the other riders to talk with Scott.

One of the stablehands took Diablo's reins from Carole and led the horse into the stable. Carole stood by as each rider dismounted, and then she and the stablehand took turns leading the horses back into their stalls. It was a fairly slow process. The last rider to dismount was Scott. She took Patch and led him to his stall. Scott followed her like a puppy. She was latching the stall door when Stevie and Lisa ran over to her.

"How was it?" Lisa asked. "Do you like being a trail leader?"

"I wasn't exactly a leader," Carole said, "and there was one little problem."

"What was the problem?" asked Lisa.

"Me," Scott said. Stevie and Lisa saw him for the first time. What they saw was a nice-looking guy with an embarrassed grin on his face who couldn't keep his eyes off their friend Carole.

"Oh, it wasn't you," Carole said. "It was Patch. Did you hear the thunder here?" She asked her friends.

"Oh, no!" Lisa said. Lisa knew firsthand what could happen to Patch when he heard a sudden loud noise. Her first day at Pine Hollow, she'd been riding Patch when somebody slammed the door. Patch didn't know

27

the difference between a slammed door and thunder. He'd taken off like a bullet. "Did you get hurt?" she asked Scott sympathetically.

"I'm okay," he said. "Thanks to Carole. She saved my life." He made the statement so dramatically that both Stevie and Lisa had to hold back their laughter.

"That's Carole, our heroine!" Stevie said. "Tell us what happened."

Scott described the events on the trail. The girls noticed the glowing terms he used to describe Carole's rescue. He used words like "daring," "bold," "heroic," "fearless," and "tremendous."

"You forgot the part about the shining armor," Stevie teased.

Scott took the ribbing good-naturedly. "I think if she'd had her armor on, she might not have moved so fast," he concluded.

"Give me a break," Carole said, more than a little embarrassed. "I really didn't do anything that wasn't expected of me—that any trained rider wouldn't have at least attempted. And it was my job to see that you came back safe and sound."

"Well, I'd like to try to make it up to you a little bit by giving you a hand around here. I mean, can I help you in some way? After all, you sure helped me."

Stevie glanced over at Carole to see what her reaction would be. Normally, Carole wouldn't want to

28

have somebody who didn't know anything about horses help her around the barn, but Scott's offer seemed so genuine and he seemed so nice.

"Oh, no thank you," Carole said. "I've just got a few little things to do, then it's time for lunch and class. Thanks for the offer anyway."

Scott looked very disappointed. "Well, I'll tell you what," he said. "My parents are taking a bus tour of the Virginia countryside tomorrow and I can't stand those things. I'm usually the youngest by at *least* forty years. I'll skip that and come back here early so I can help you with your morning chores, okay? Then you can tell me more about riding. I like to hear you talk about it."

"Okay," Carole relented. "But I warn you, morning chores aren't always exactly fun."

"It doesn't matter," Scott told her. "See you then." He waved good-bye to all three girls, but his eyes never left Carole. She waved back and then turned her attention to Patch. He needed some fresh water in his bucket.

"At least you have until tomorrow," Stevie said.

"To do what?" Carole asked her.

"To polish up your armor, of course!" Stevie said. Then she and Lisa burst into laughter.

"Don't be silly," Carole said.

"Who's being silly?" Stevie asked. "He's madly in

love with you—and he's *cute,* too. I love those dark brown eyes. They practically sparkled when they looked at you—and they looked at you a lot, did you notice?"

"Not really," Carole said, carrying the bucket to the faucet. Then she added, "Well, sort of. You think he's got a thing for me?"

Stevie nodded vigorously.

"He's a nice-enough guy," Carole said. "And he is kind of cute, but I don't think he's my type."

"Just because he doesn't know anything about horses?" Lisa asked. "It certainly doesn't mean he can't learn. Look at me."

"And he's eager enough," Stevie reminded her.

Carole slipped the big plastic bucket under the faucet and turned it on full force. Fresh, cool water rushed in, rinsing out the dust that always accumulated. Carole sloshed the water around in the bucket, dumped it out, and then put some water in it for Patch. She returned to the horse's stall, her two friends trailing her.

"Oh, he's eager, all right, but he just doesn't seem like my type."

"Oh, really? And just what *is* your type?" Stevie teased.

Lisa giggled. "And if those looks of glowing admiration mean anything, you're going to have a rough time convincing him you're not *his* type."

"Yeah, I know," Carole said. "I've already been thinking about how to do it," she admitted.

"It's not easy," Lisa said. She recalled the rough time she had had when Stevie's brother Chad developed a crush on her and it had turned out they didn't have anything in common. At least he had come to the same conclusion, though, so it wasn't really difficult. In this case she could see that it might not be so easy.

"Hey, I've got an idea," Stevie said. "If Scott's going to be here all day tomorrow, why don't you put him to work on chores—like he asked."

"He'd probably love it," Carole said. "And what good would that do me?" She hung up Patch's bucket, and while the tired horse took his first long slurp, she left the stall and latched it closed.

"Maybe you're right," Stevie said. "But then again, maybe there's more to chores than meets the eye. Come on. It's time for lunch. Let's get our sandwiches and talk about a plan."

Carole and Lisa looked at each other. When Stevie got like this, it meant something was up—and the something was usually worth waiting for.

Eagerly, they followed her to the tack room, where there was a small refrigerator for their lunch bags.

They retrieved them and each took a soda from the ample supply Max always kept there. Stevie led them to their favorite lunch spot—a knoll overlooking the paddock where Delilah and her colt, Samson, spent their afternoons. Today, in the heat, the two horses were standing idly in a shady corner, evading flies.

Stevie unwrapped her tuna fish sandwich and opened her soda with a flourish.

"Okay, so what's your idea?" Carole challenged her.

"Well, soaping saddles and lugging buckets of water are just one part of horse care, aren't they?" she asked.

Carole and Lisa agreed.

"Max has been complaining a lot recently about how carelessly some of the students have been mucking out the stables," Stevie continued with a sly smile. "It would be a good idea to just spend a whole day at it. If you really took the time, you could clean out every single smelly corner. But we're all so busy. If only there were *someone* else who could help out . . ."

Lisa burst out laughing, but Carole's expression was serious as she put her chin in her hand and stared at her bologna-and-cheese sandwich. "Mucking out? *All* day long? He'd never want to look at another horse—or me—as long as he lives."

"That's what you have in mind, isn't it?" Lisa asked. She knew that Stevie's idea was brilliant, as most of Stevie's ideas were.

Carole took a bite of her sandwich and chewed thoughtfully. "I think you might have something there," she said, finally smiling. "I'll even let him use the new pitchfork!"

"You're all heart!" Lisa joked. They all laughed, thinking about what was in store for Scott the next day.

"Is this another joke about a talking dog?" Carole asked her father at breakfast the next morning.

The colonel nodded eagerly. "And one of the best, too," he assured her. Next to fifties and sixties music, Colonel Hanson's favorite subject was old jokes. Usually, the colonel swapped them with Stevie, who seemed to love them as much as he did, but since Stevie wasn't there, he told this one to his daughter instead.

"So this man makes a ten-dollar bet with a stranger that his dog can talk. He asks the dog what goes on top of a house and the dog says 'Roof!' The stranger shakes his head. The man asks his dog what sandpaper is like. The dog says 'Rough!' The stranger won't pay up. Then the man asks the dog who was the greatest baseball player of all time. The dog says 'Ruth!' The stranger still refuses to pay, so the man and his dog walk away. While they're walking, the man turns to his dog and says, 'You just cost me ten bucks, you know!' The dog looks at him. 'What did you want me to say,' the dog asks, 'Joe diMaggio?'"

Carole laughed in spite of herself. "I think I've heard it before," she told her father, "but it's still good. Want me to tell Stevie?"

"No," the colonel said. "I'll tell her myself the next time she calls. You want some more bacon?" He stood up to help himself to seconds.

"No, I'm fine. I'm going to have a busy day at the stable, so I don't want to start out too full."

"Really? What's up?" he asked.

"Oh, it's a long story," Carole said. "But—" She was interrupted by the ringing of the phone.

"Why don't you answer it?" the colonel asked. "It's usually for you."

When Carole answered, she was a little disappointed to hear the voice of Lynne Blessing. "Oh, hi, how are you?" Carole asked automatically. Lynne was a woman her father had been dating recently. Since her mother's death the year before, Carole had always encouraged her father to date. She liked the idea of him having fun with new friends because she had so much fun with her own friends.

The trouble was that Lynne wasn't what she'd had in mind.

Not only did she interfere by trying to drive Carole places—and making her late, as she had been to Pine Hollow the day before—but she always seemed to want to meddle in Carole's life. It was as if Lynne thought she ought to make some changes in Carole. And she was at it again.

"Oh, I'm so glad to talk to you, Carole," Lynne bubbled over the telephone. "There's a sale going on at The Dress Rack at the mall. They have some of the most wonderful things. I was hoping you'd like to go with me. We could have fun shopping together. Just us girls, you know. Wouldn't that be fun?"

Carole pasted a smile on her face. Even though Lynne couldn't see it, it would help her pretend she was being nice, and it might fool her father, too. Going to the mall with Lynne would take a *lot* of pretending. Lynne's idea of a pretty dress included ruffles, lace, and bows. Carole's idea of a pretty dress was a comfortable pair of jeans. Carole still hadn't figured out how to wear the scarf Lynne had given her a month earlier.

"I'm afraid I'm busy that day, Lynne," Carole said. It sounded polite.

"Which day?" Lynne asked. "We could go on Saturday or any afternoon next week."

"Here's Dad," Carole said, ducking the question. She handed the phone to her father. While he chatted pleasantly with Lynne, Carole collected the dishes and put them in the sink to soak. She wiped off the breakfast table and then, popping an apple into her lunch bag for dessert, she checked her watch and waved good-bye to her father. If the bus was on schedule, she had just two and a half minutes to make it—and if she didn't make that one, she'd certainly have to talk to Lynne some more. The door slammed behind her and she dashed to the corner.

CAROLE ARRIVED AT the stable early. And so did Scott. He was standing by the entrance waiting for her when she walked up the driveway.

"Good morning," he said brightly.

And it was. It was a beautiful summer day with a bright blue sky and not a hint of clouds. All signs of the storm of the previous day were gone. This was the kind of day to be out on the trail, not indoors doing chores.

"Hi," Carole said to Scott. She swung her equipment bag up over her shoulder. "You sure you still want to do this?" she asked.

"Do what?" he asked suspiciously.

"Whatever chores I'm going to do," she said to him.

"Yup," he assured her.

"Okay, then. Follow me," she said. First she led him into Max's office, where she got clearance to cut classes for the day to work on cleaning the stalls. Max could hardly believe that she was suggesting it, but he agreed, readily.

Then Scott followed her into the tack room. After they both changed into work boots, she had Scott haul out the pitchforks, shovels, and utility carts. Then they began their task. It wasn't a pleasant one.

First, Carole removed a horse from its stall and secured him in the aisle of the stable. Then, while she hauled the fresh peat and straw from the storage area in a cart, Scott was in charge of removing all of the soiled straw and muck and shoveling it into another cart. There was a lot of it.

Carole had to admit that Scott was a hard worker. While she hauled away the first load of refuse in one cart, he filled another. As fast as she could dump them, he could fill them. But it was hard work. When the stall was finally emptied, Scott squirted in the cleanser and brushed down the inside, finishing up with a good hosing. Most stalls had manure removed a couple of times a day and fresh straw would be added as necessary. But every once in a while it was necessary to clean them from the bottom up, and Carole discovered that Scott was a championship cleaner.

"Hey, you don't have to work quite so hard," she said. "You want to take a break?"

"Oh, no!" he told her. "Let's finish up this stall so we can get on to the next one."

Carole couldn't believe it. She stared at him with her mouth open.

"You tired?" he asked.

She was, but there was no way she would admit it.

Usually, it took an hour or so to do a thorough cleaning of each stall. Scott was going at such speed that he'd finished one in less than a half hour.

Carole's frequent trips to the manure pile did not go unnoticed by Max. In between his classes, he came over to her.

"What's going on in there?" he asked. "You got a team of workers shoveling for you?"

"Just one," she said. "Best worker I ever saw, too."

"I'm going to have to see this," he said.

"You're going to have to see it to *believe* it, you mean," she said. He followed her inside the stable.

Max watched in amazement as Scott finished up his third stall. Carole shoveled in the new peat and fresh straw and smoothed it all around the floor of the stall before returning the horse.

"Never saw a better worker," Max said. "He's something."

Carole had to agree with that. The only trouble was

that it was clear Stevie's brainstorm was a total failure. Scott was as happy as a clam to be shoveling manure. By the end of the day, when they'd mucked out a lot of stalls, he was looking around for more.

"That's all that needs to be done now," she told him. He looked very disappointed.

"It's probably just as well," he said. "I'm supposed to meet my folks for a nighttime tour of the city in about an hour. I probably ought to shower first, don't you think so?"

Carole giggled and nodded.

"Okay, then, I'll be back tomorrow," he said cheerfully.

"There's no riding camp tomorrow," she said. "It's Saturday."

"Oh," he said, clearly disappointed. "Will you be back here Monday?"

Carole sighed, mostly to herself. "I'll be here," she told him. "But I'll be in class all day."

"Maybe I can watch?"

"Maybe," she said noncommittally. "So long."

She watched him walk down the driveway that led away from the stables. His shoulders were rounded with fatigue and his head drooped forward. But for some reason, there was still a spring in his step. Carole shook her head in surprise. Scott was really quite a boy. She admired the way he had attacked the cleaning chore and gotten the unpleasant job done. She'd even enjoyed his company as they worked together. But the summer was for horses, not boyfriends, she thought, heading for a much-needed shower herself. She really wasn't interested in going out yet, even with a nice boy like Scott.

"HE MUCKED OUT *how* many stalls today?" Stevie asked Carole.

"Didn't you hear Max talking about him to Red?" Lisa asked. "Said he'd never seen a better stable worker!"

"You know what this means, don't you?" Carole asked Stevie. "It means your plan didn't work and you've got to come up with something else!"

The girls were sitting at a booth at Tastee Delight —or TD's, as the ice cream parlor at the local shopping center was called. The three members of The Saddle Club met there frequently for treats after riding. They called such gatherings Saddle Club meetings because the subject was usually horses. Today, however, the subject was Scott.

"Oh, there are lots of other things you can do," Stevie assured her.

"Like what?" Carole challenged.

"The first thing you do is start talking about your other boyfriends," Stevie advised.

"I don't have any," Carole reminded her.

"But he doesn't know that," Lisa said.

"I can't do that. I wouldn't know what to say."

"Okay, okay," Stevie said. "Here's another idea. Talk too much. Bore him to death by talking about horses. You can do *that*, can't you?"

Carole glanced at Stevie. "Very funny. Besides, I already *do*. He hangs on every word I say. Today, I was talking about colic. You should have heard me go on about it. He even wanted to hear the part about milk of magnesia!"

"Oh, yuck!" Stevie said, putting her spoon back down on her plate. "Nobody likes that part."

"You're right," Carole agreed. "You two would have shut me up long before I got to that!"

Stevie and Lisa smiled. It was true that Carole was prone to talking about horses too much—and in too much detail. It was hard to imagine anybody listening to her complete discussion of a horse's digestive problems!

"Okay, then, be boring about something else. Tell him you have a really dull hobby. I have a nerdy cousin who collects beer cans. Want to try that?"

"Wouldn't work," Carole said. "*He* collects matchbook covers."

"Bugs? Want to tell him you have a bug collection?"

"No way. He'd probably ask to see it."

"There *must* be a way," Stevie insisted.

"Yeah," Lisa agreed.

"Sure," Carole concluded. "But what *is* it?"

STEVIE WAS SO excited she could barely dial the phone. "Did Jackie Small just call you?" she blurted out when Lisa answered on the first ring.

"Boy, did she ever!" Lisa said. "And it took a whole bunch of convincing to get my mom to agree. You know how she can be, don't you?"

"Yeah, but she did agree, didn't she? I mean that's the important thing."

"Only when I promised her that I'd agree to the piano lessons she wants me to take in the fall."

"Whew!" Stevie said. "I was really afraid she'd say no."

"Me, too," Lisa said. "But she didn't and this is the most exciting thing that's ever happened to me."

"Me, too."

Stevie leaned back on the pillows on her bed, relaxing for a good long phone conversation with Lisa. There was a lot to talk about.

Jackie Small wanted both of the girls to work for her in a photo session the next day. She had called to say that she had finished developing her pictures and she was sure both Stevie and Lisa would do exceptionally well. Jackie wanted them to help her with a catalog "shoot" for both English and western riding clothes and equipment. And, best of all, she was actually going to *pay* them!

"This is only the beginning, you know," Stevie said. She twirled the phone cord around her fingers as she got caught up in the excitement.

"What do you mean?" Lisa asked.

"Well, all models start with little jobs like this, but the thing is, see, if you've got the kind of face and figure that photograph well . . ." Her words hung in the air for a few seconds.

"You mean you think this could lead to other jobs?"

"Lily Logan had to start someplace, didn't she?"

"Who?"

"Lily Logan—she's this famous model," Stevie reminded her friend.

"Oh, like on the makeup commercial!" Lisa said, remembering it from television. A cool summer breeze wafted into her room. She could feel her hair being brushed back by the puff of wind. In her imagination she was on a sailboat, in a sleek white cotton outfit, holding the mast casually with one hand while being refreshed by the light wind and the salty mist. *Smile! Click! That's a take!*

"You think Lily Logan did a catalog for riding clothes?" Lisa asked.

"When you just start out, like us, you'll do anything," Stevie said. "You've got to have something to fill your portfolio—until the offers start coming over the phone." Stevie squeezed the telephone cord. It became the handle of a large portfolio filled with luscious pictures of herself in sports clothes, evening clothes, school clothes. Her favorite portfolio shot showed her at a school basketball game, completely surrounded by the team!

"It's a lot of money, isn't it?" Lisa asked, interrupting Stevie's daydream.

"Oh, it's *nothing* compared to what the big-time models get. But just wait . . ."

As she stepped to the edge of the sidewalk, Stevie's chauffeur swept the door open in front of her, and, at the same time, unburdened her of all the packages she was carrying. He also held her toy poodle by the leash.

"And you know what else models do—a *lot* of traveling," Stevie said.

"You mean like to Europe and Asia and Africa . . ."

Lisa looked out the window at the sky streaked pink by the setting sun. Nine o'clock at home meant two o'clock in the morning in Monte Carlo. She was driving back to her hotel from the casino in a red two-seater sports car. The top was down. The moonlight gleamed on the Mediterranean below, sparkling across the warm waters where only this afternoon she had been swimming with the duke.

"And we'll learn all about makeup and fashions," Stevie said, breaking into Lisa's daydream.

"And we'll be friends, no matter what happens!" Lisa vowed. "I mean even if I get more and better jobs than you do—"

"What makes you think you *will*?" Stevie asked. "Jackie told me she thought I'd be just *perfect* for this job. I'm sure I will be for lots of others, too."

"Funny, that's the same thing she said to me. I just didn't know she'd said it to you, too. I didn't want to hurt your feelings."

"How could you hurt my feelings when we're going to be the first two girls from Willow Creek, Virginia, to appear on the cover of *Vogue* together!"

"And we'll have to go to *Paris* for the shoot, won't we?" Lisa had already picked up some of the language of photography. She really liked using the word "shoot."

So did Stevie.

"Definitely Paris for the *Vogue* shoot, but I guess it's

plain old Willow Creek for the *Young Rider's* catalog."

"It's just a start," Lisa reminded her. "We have to begin someplace. As long as we stick together, we'll be fine, too."

"Uh, Lisa," Stevie said. "About Carole . . ."

"Yeah, I know," Lisa said.

"I asked Jackie."

"So did I," Lisa said. "And she told me you'd already asked her."

"Yeah. I told her that she was missing out on the best rider in the school. At first, she thought I meant Veronica, but I explained about Carole."

"I know. But she told me she could only afford two of us to work for the catalog."

All of the fun dreams disappeared. "It doesn't seem right," Stevie said. "She should be in on the fun, too."

"We can invite her along to Monte Carlo," Lisa said.

"Monte Carlo?" asked Stevie.

"I guess I was daydreaming," Lisa confessed. "I was imagining a moonlit beach and sparkling water and this neat red sports car . . ."

"And a gorgeous guy?"

"Well . . ." Both girls giggled.

"But what about Carole?"

"We've got to tell her," Lisa said.

"Of course we do, but telling isn't enough. After all,

she just spent an entire day mucking out stalls with a guy who collects matchbook covers, and you and I are talking about modeling in Paris. Not only do we have to tell her, but we have to make it up to her!"

"Sure, but how?" Lisa asked.

"I don't know," Stevie said. "But I'll think of something."

"I hope whatever you think of works better than your last brainstorm," Lisa said.

"It will," Stevie assured her. "I promise."

"I've got to go," Lisa said hastily. "My mom's coming upstairs and I'm supposed to be doing my summer reading. See you on Saturday!"

"Okay, bye," Stevie said. She cradled the phone and leaned back against the soft pillows. She looked up at the ceiling. The shadows cast by her lampshade looked like a map. A map of the world. Hong Kong, Tokyo, Buenos Aires, Nepal, Amsterdam, Calcutta, Sydney. Images of exotic places danced before her eyes, places she had never dreamed of going before, places she had barely even heard of! Her heart beat fast with excitement.

But there was something wrong. And she knew what it was: What would they say to Carole?

"DID YOU BRING the makeup?" Stevie asked Lisa eagerly when they met at the stable's locker room on Saturday morning.

"Makeup, makeup, what's that?" Lisa asked, rubbing her eyes sleepily. "It's too early in the morning to remember *anything.*"

It was, in fact, six-thirty in the morning. Jackie had told the girls to be at Pine Hollow and ready to begin the shoot by seven. The morning sun was the best for photography, and anyway, it was going to be awfully hot by noon.

"Makeup," Stevie repeated. "If we're going to show ourselves off to our best advantage, we've got to be wearing makeup. You *promised* you'd bring it."

"Of course I brought it," Lisa said, hefting a large

case to the bench. "After all, you only called me about it three times."

"Well, my mother hardly ever wears it, so I didn't know what I might be able to borrow from her. But *your* mother—"

"My mother wouldn't be seen in public without perfectly applied makeup," Lisa finished for her. Lisa's mother believed that what other people thought of her was Very Important. "I think the mailman once delivered something before she'd put on her makeup. She hasn't been able to face him since!"

"Very funny," Stevie said. "By the way, I tried to call Carole, but I chickened out!"

"Me, too," Lisa admitted with a sheepish smile as Stevie snapped open Lisa's case, which held a large variety of creams, pencils, and powders.

"What are we supposed to do with this stuff?" Stevie asked, suddenly overwhelmed.

Lisa's eyes lit with mischief. "We are supposed to transform ourselves into international beauties!"

"Well, then, let's not waste a minute," Stevie said, giggling. She reached for a bottle and opened it. "What's this for?" she asked suspiciously, sniffing at the white cream. It smelled nice enough, but it didn't look like it was going to transform her.

"I think that's wrinkle cream," Lisa said.

"I don't need any wrinkles," Stevie told her.

51

"It's to keep you from *getting* any, dummy."

"Oh. They'd be bad for a model, wouldn't they? I'd better put some on." She tilted the bottle until a gooey glob of wrinkle cream filled her palm. She smeared it on her face. "It's really oily. Do I look better?"

Lisa examined her friend's face. "I think the long-term effect may be worth it, but for now, all that's happened is that your face looks greasy."

"That's what I was afraid you were going to say." She grabbed a tissue and tried to wipe the stuff off. It only smeared it. "I'll go wash it off," she announced, standing up.

While Stevie went into the bathroom to wash off the wrinkle cream, Lisa examined the possibilities in front of her. She applied some liquid makeup, but the results were streaks that made her look suspiciously like an Indian on the warpath. She wiped it off. She was carefully drawing light brown eyebrows on herself when Stevie reappeared.

"It doesn't come off." Stevie was trying to sound calm, but Lisa could hear the panic in her voice.

Lisa looked over her shoulder in the mirror and then spun around to look directly at her friend. Stevie's face was as greasy as it had been before she washed it.

"How am I ever going to be a glamorous fashion model with gooey guck on my face!" Stevie wailed.

"Don't worry, we'll think of something," Lisa said

quickly, trying to sound reassuring. "There must be something here." She began digging through the jars and tubes in the case. "Magic wand? No, that's for eyelashes. Here's some nail-polish remover. That ought to do it." She read the label. "Oops, that stuff's poisonous. Creme de something-or-other. Sounds like a dessert—not a makeup remover." Lisa giggled. "Skin buffer? I don't know what it does, but if we buff you, you're going to shine for months!"

"Lisa!" Stevie wailed. "*Do* something!"

"I can't," Lisa announced. "There's nothing here that says it's going to remove that stuff from your face."

"I'll *never* be able to be a model with this stuff on. And if I blow it on this job, I may never have another opportunity!"

"Well, there could be a future for you modeling ski masks," Lisa suggested.

"Grrr," Stevie said, and Lisa had the feeling she was seriously upset. "I'll solve my own problem," Stevie declared. She spun on her heel and left Lisa alone.

Lisa regarded the remaining selection of makeup warily. She had thought putting on makeup would be fun, but it was turning out to be hazardous. It just wasn't a job for amateurs. Besides, Jackie hadn't said anything about it. In fact, Jackie had told both girls that they didn't need to bring anything. She was going to supply them with everything required. That proba-

bly included makeup. Lisa hoped it included something to remove the greasy cream from Stevie's face.
She carefully replaced all of her mother's cosmetics in
the case and clicked it shut. It would be a couple of
years before she was ready to tackle that task again—
even if she did become a world-famous fashion model.

Lisa heard Stevie's footsteps behind her. She was
afraid to look. She was afraid to ask.

"It worked," Stevie announced. Lisa turned around
slowly. There stood Stevie, looking just like Stevie
usually looked, pretty shoulder-length blond hair sur-
rounding a nice oval face, which *wasn't* covered with
goo.

"How'd you do it?" Lisa asked.

"I'll tell you later," Stevie said with a mischievous
grin. "But right now, Jackie's here and it's time to get to
work."

"Good morning, girls!" Jackie Small called brightly
from the stable door. "Are we ready?"

"You bet we are!" they answered in chorus.

Both Stevie and Lisa were practically shivering with
excitement. They were on the brink of exotic new
lives!

A FEW HOURS after Stevie and Lisa had tried to transform themselves into glamorous models, Lynne Blessing was trying to transform Carole into something

else. Carole found herself wishing she were back at Pine Hollow mucking out stables with Scott.

Instead, she was at the mall with Lynne Blessing.

Lynne had been nothing but nice, caring, and attentive since they had left Carole's house. But still Carole wished she were anywhere but there. Maybe it was because Lynne was just trying too hard.

"Oh, Carole!" Lynne gushed. "I just love those little roses, don't you?"

Carole looked at herself in the mirror in the store's dressing room. What she saw dismayed her. She had never owned anything with little roses on it and she didn't want to start now. The dress Lynne had selected for Carole to try on was made of pink chiffon over taffeta. It had a blousy top with a scalloped white collar, short sleeves, and a big white bow around the waist. A big red rose, matching the "little roses" in the fabric, emerged from the middle of the bow. The short sleeves had white cuffs.

"I think I look like a Kewpie doll," Carole said flatly. "It's just really not me, Lynne."

"Oh, but it's *darling*," Lynne tried to reassure her. Carole was not convinced. Lynne had brought piles of dresses for Carole to try on and all of them were just plain wrong. Carole didn't like frilly, lacy dresses. In fact, what Carole liked to wear were jeans, and Lynne hadn't gotten within a quarter of a mile of the jeans stores at the mall. Besides, Carole couldn't imagine *where* she would wear one of these frilly things.

"These dresses are nice and all, but they're really not the kind of thing I like to wear much," Carole told Lynne as nicely as she could. She was trying very hard to be polite, but it wasn't easy. Her father had absolutely *made* her come shopping with Lynne. Carole couldn't remember the last time her father had put his foot down like that. She realized that for some reason, this was important to him. Since it was important to him, she was trying awfully hard to make it work.

"I think I saw something else on the rack that you might like, then," Lynne said. "You slip out of that and I'll get that other one I saw. It's just *so* pretty, Carole. Wait a sec, okay?"

"Okay," Carole said. The suspense was killing her. Violets, maybe, this time? Or just plain lace? Would it have the frilly stuff at the neck or at the hem? Carole stepped out of the number with the little roses, and awaited Lynne's return.

In a few minutes, Lynne knocked at the dressing room door. She was once again laden down with dresses. Carole couldn't imagine how so many manufacturers could have gotten together to make so many ugly dresses at the same time. Actually, to be honest, a lot of them really weren't ugly. It was just that they weren't right for Carole.

"Now here's the new selection," Lynne announced.

"I think I already tried that one on," Carole said, pointing to a pale purple creation she had despised. Lynne held up a yellow dress with a very frilly collar. "Looks like a clown collar," Carole commented flatly.

"I guess it does at that," Lynne said, critically examining the dress. "I just don't seem to be doing very well for you, Carole." She looked so disappointed that Carole began to feel a little sorry for her. She didn't want to hurt Lynne's feelings, but she didn't want to have to wear something with printed pastel flowers on it, either.

"What's that one?" Carole asked, tugging gently at some white cotton she spotted in the midst of the garden of dresses Lynne held.

"I don't know if it's right, but I thought maybe . . ." Lynne said uncertainly.

Carole quickly stowed most of Lynne's latest choices on the "no" hook in the dressing room, and then held the white cotton up to herself. It was a plain dress compared to the others. It had a snug bodice with a V neck surrounded by an eyelet lace shawl collar. The straps were on the edge of the shoulders. The dress had a full skirt made of plain white cotton, with eyelet lace trim at the hem.

"I think I'll try this one on," Carole said. Lynne's face lit up with joy. Carole could tell that Lynne was happy to have found something Carole *wanted* to try on. Carole slipped the dress over her head and stood still in front of the mirror while Lynne zipped it up the back. In fact, Carole hated having somebody zip her dress for her, but Lynne seemed to need to do it, so Carole didn't protest.

When Lynne stood back, Carole examined her reflection. It wasn't bad. The dress fit well, showing off her nice figure, but not *too* much. She twirled and the puffy skirt flared.

"Not bad," Carole said. She turned so that her back was to the mirror and looked over her shoulder. The neckline made a V in the back, matching the one in the front. It was kind of pretty.

"Oh, I *love* it!" Lynne exclaimed. "You must have it. Okay, then, since that's decided, why don't you get back into your regular clothes and I'll go pay for this, then we'll stop at the coffee shop next to the shoe store and have a cup of tea, or whatever you'd like, before we buy you a pair of shoes to go with this? What fun we'll have! I have a white clutch purse you could borrow if you'd like and you know what would look good? I have a luscious pink shawl you could kind of throw over your shoulders . . ."

Carole shuddered.

"CAN YOU LEAN back a little bit farther, Lisa?" Jackie asked.

Lisa thought she was already leaning back so far that she must look very silly. She was grasping the edge of a saddle. The saddle was tilted over a saddle rack so that more than half the saddle would show at once. Lisa was practically lying on the ground.

"I'm afraid I'll get all dirty," Lisa said.

"That's all right," Jackie assured her, snapping away furiously. Then she said, "I think I'd better try to get another set of the same saddle without the sunlight gleaming on it. Can you turn the rack and get down on the other side?"

Other side? That meant she was going to be completely out of view of the camera. She crawled up out of the dirt, turned the rack until Jackie said it was okay, and then slunk down in the dirt again, keeping the saddle from falling forward while Jackie photographed it.

"It's a take!" Jackie said—the very words Lisa had been daydreaming about yesterday. But yesterday's dreams had included wind in her hair—not dirt.

"Now, girls," Jackie said. "Let's do those boots. Lisa, you do the jodhpur boots with the elastic ankle. Stevie, get the black pair of high boots."

"What else should we wear?" Stevie asked.

"What you've got on is fine," Jackie said.

Stevie looked down. She was wearing her Washington Redskins T-shirt over her riding jeans. That would look very funny with the fancy riding boots. She and Lisa exchanged looks. Lisa was trying to brush the dirt from her blouse. It wasn't coming off.

"This is going to be a strange catalog," Lisa whispered. "I never saw one with the models lying in the dirt behind the saddle before, did you?"

"Nope," Stevie agreed. "But she seems to know exactly what she wants, so let's do it."

The girls and Jackie had been working in the hot sun in a small paddock behind the Pine Hollow barn all morning. Jackie had all of her equipment with her, including the clothes, saddles, bridles, boots, and hats to be photographed. Saturday was usually a very busy day at Pine Hollow, but they were out of the way of the weekend traffic. In fact, they hadn't even seen Max or Red O'Malley since they had arrived.

Stevie tried to put on the boots. She got her toe in okay, and then her heel, but she couldn't pull them up at all. She looked at the label. No wonder. They were two sizes too small for her!

"Jackie, I can't get my feet into these things!" she called out of the dressing area.

"It doesn't matter," Jackie assured her casually.

"It does to me," Stevie said, rolling her eyes upward. She tugged harder. She found that she could get her toe into the foot of the boot, though of course, the boot looked silly with her jeans anyway, since it was meant to be worn with breeches. But if she stood on the balls of her feet, and if she held onto a wall or fence, she could walk. Like a duck. She waddled out into the photographic area.

Lisa held her hand so she wouldn't fall over. But it wasn't easy. *Her* boots were a men's size and she shuffled along in them, nearly leaving them behind her with every step.

"Oh, don't get them dusty, girls!" Jackie said. "Come on now, take them off and rub them until they shine. I think if we put them up against the white fence, it'll show them off well. Make sure they're on grass."

While the girls hobbled over to the grassy area by the fence, Jackie changed filters and lenses.

"Did she say 'take them off'?" Lisa asked.

"I hope so," Stevie said. "Because I'm about to fall over." And with that, she did. Lisa tugged the tight boots off Stevie's feet and finished brushing the dust off them. Lisa set the boots aside until Stevie could stand to put them on again. Then, without meaning to, she stepped out of the jodhpur boots she was wearing and fell smack onto the ground with a thud. She was going to have a nasty bruise on her elbow where she had landed.

"Good thing it wasn't scraped," Lisa said. "That wouldn't look at all pretty in the photographs, would it?"

"No, it wouldn't, but I'm beginning to wonder if it matters," Stevie said.

"What do you mean?" Lisa asked her.

"Well, I've never worked harder in my life. I thought I was going to die from heat exhaustion when I was holding the horse with the western saddle. It must have taken Jackie an hour to do that one photograph."

"Now, wait a minute," Lisa said. "I know you had a rough time with that, but remember I was sitting *in* the saddle for that one. And the saddle didn't fit me at all."

"Neither did the cowboy boots you were wearing," Stevie reminded her sympathetically. "But they fit better than the ones I just took off!"

Jackie approached the fence, camera ready.

"I bet she wants us to put those things back on now," Lisa said. "Ugh." She turned. "Ready for us, Jackie?" she asked.

"Perfect, just perfect," Jackie was saying to nobody in particular. Her camera was already clicking away. When Lisa looked at the target, she found it was the two pairs of boots in front of the white fence. There was nobody in them. No models. That was Jackie's idea of perfect. It was beginning to be Lisa's idea of perfect, too.

"Next, we do halters," Jackie announced, reloading her camera.

Halters meant using more horses. Stevie and Lisa spent the next hour holding horses so that their heads were pointed just right for Jackie, showing off the different kinds of halters.

"I think I'm getting the picture here," Stevie said, standing next to Comanche on the side away from the camera. The horse was wearing a pretty red nylon halter with a brass nameplate. The halter was a size too large for the horse. Stevie's job was to grasp it just enough to make it look as though it fit him.

"I don't think you're in the picture at all," Lisa said.

She was standing off to the side, facing Comanche. It was her job to get Comanche's attention when Jackie wanted him to look up.

"*That's* the point," Stevie told her. "Jackie's gotten a couple of good photographs of my hands, two of your feet. One of your arm when you were holding the reins, two of mine, which she didn't want, when Comanche shook his head. Other than that, we're not in these pictures at all."

"You mean we're not really models?" Lisa asked.

"That's exactly what I mean."

"Maybe *that's* why we're not having any fun," Lisa said.

"No, I think it would be worse if we were models. We would have *had* to wear those boots!"

"No wonder models get paid so much!" Lisa said. "They get paid a lot more than we're getting—and it's still not enough!"

Lisa shook her head. She hated the idea of her dream vanishing into thin air, but that seemed to be exactly what was happening. So much for Monte Carlo, Paris, and the cover of *Vogue*. If she couldn't take a day at Pine Hollow, there was no way she could stand a life of modeling.

"What time is it?" she asked.

"Lunchtime," Stevie said. She turned to Jackie. "Can we break for lunch?"

"Oh, no!" Jackie said. "I've got another line to photograph and the sky's looking iffy. No way can we stop!"

Stevie sighed. She and Lisa had made a deal with Jackie and they weren't going to break their word. "Okay, come on, Lisa. I think we're doing blankets next."

"Great. Comanche's going to love having a blanket on now that it's only practically broiling hot outside," Lisa complained.

"Right, and it's your turn to hold the horse. You're going to love being under the blanket with him, holding him still so the blanket doesn't slide off!"

"You wouldn't, would you?" Lisa asked.

Stevie would.

WHEN CAROLE FINISHED changing back into her own jeans, she followed Lynne out of the dressing room and waited while she paid for the dress. After the saleswoman handed Carole the bag, Lynne marched happily out of the shop. Carole trailed her through the maze of teenagers, parents, and crying children in the crowded local shopping mall. Lynne chatted on about the total outfit she was building around the dress she'd bought for Carole. Carole knew that sooner or later she was going to hear about some flowers, for a color accent, but at least she'd found a dress she could stand

and that seemed to make Lynne happy. And making Lynne happy would make her father happy. And when the colonel was happy, Carole was happy.

Soon, the two of them spotted the coffee shop; Lynne was *still* talking about Carole's outfit when they sat down at their table. Carole ordered a root beer. Lynne ordered iced tea. Then she returned to her favorite subject: Carole's new dress.

"You know, Carole, I have a beautiful grosgrain ribbon with bright red roses. It will look wonderful in your curly hair, and the red of the roses will go nicely with the pink shawl. You'll be the belle of the ball."

"Belle of the ball? What do you mean?" Carole asked, suddenly very suspicious.

"At the dance next week, of course," Lynne said.

"What dance?"

"The one on the base. Your father talked with you about it, didn't he?"

Carole frowned and shook her head. She knew that some kids hardly ever talked with their parents, but she and her father talked a lot. For example, he had told her another old joke this morning. He had told her that there was a bird's nest blocking their porch light. He had told her they were out of popcorn and would need more today, since one of his favorite old movies, *The D.I.*, was on television tonight, but he hadn't said a thing about a dance at the base next week.

"This is news to me," Carole told Lynne, a funny feeling growing in the pit of her stomach.

"Mitch can be funny sometimes, can't he?"

"Yes, he can," Carole agreed, but she didn't think this was one of them. She was not amused.

"It's a fund-raiser for Toys for Tots at the Officers' Club at the base on Saturday night. Your dad has taken a table for four. You'll need a date, of course, but I'm sure a pretty girl like you has a lot of young men who are just dying to date you."

Carole could barely believe what she was hearing. It was getting worse and worse! "Not exactly," she said to Lynne. "And there aren't any *I'm* dying to date, and I didn't know anything at all about this dance, and nobody's asked me if *I* want to go—" Carole was so angry she was practically sputtering, but Lynne didn't seem to notice at all.

"Oh, no, you're going to have to ask the boy, Carole. A boy couldn't ask *you* to this, unless, of course, his family had bought tickets, and we're counting on you being at *our* table, dear."

Carole's soda arrived. She looked at it glumly and sighed. Obviously, being nice to Lynne meant not only letting her buy a dress, but also agreeing to go along to this dance thing. No wonder her father hadn't told her about it. He *knew* she wouldn't want to go!

She would mount an argument all right, but there was no point in arguing with Lynne. This woman, with all her good intentions, didn't seem to understand Carole at all. Carole pierced the top of her soda with her straw and drank a big gulp of it. She would argue, all right, but it wouldn't be with Lynne. She would argue with her father. He would understand.

LISA STRETCHED OUT on the bench in the locker room. "I just heard the most wonderful noise in the world," she announced.

"What was that?" Stevie asked, lying on the other end of the bench so that they were head-to-head.

"The sound of Jackie's truck pulling away from Pine Hollow. Can you believe this day? I never worked harder in my life!"

"What I can't believe is that we thought it was going to be fun."

"Glamorous."

"Exciting."

"Instead, it was boring and exhausting," Lisa said. "I think I've decided that I definitely don't want to be a model. We didn't even have a chance to learn anything about makeup!"

"I learned everything I ever wanted to know about

makeup this morning," Stevie said, reminding Lisa of the disaster of the wrinkle cream.

"Yeah, and you were going to tell me how you finally got that stuff off."

Stevie laughed.

"What's so funny?" Lisa asked her. "What *did* you do?"

"I used an old, familiar standby. Something you can always find around here."

"You didn't!" Lisa said.

"Yep, I did. I used saddle soap. Worked like a dream."

Lisa began giggling along with Stevie. That was a nice way to end a very long day.

"OF COURSE I understand, honey," the colonel said to Carole a few hours later when they were alone at home. Lynne had stayed for dinner and had left around eight-thirty. Carole had remained quiet about the dance until Lynne was out of the house, but then she had turned to her father for an explanation. He understood, all right, but it didn't make any difference. "But it still doesn't change things. Lynne seems to think it's very important that you be with us that night, so we'll do it her way. That's my decision. And it's final."

"Da-ad!" Carole complained. "You didn't even have the guts to tell me about it!"

"Guilty!" he said with a sheepish smile. "I knew you wouldn't like the idea if you heard it from me. But Lynne's so enthusiastic I assumed it would sound better coming from her."

"You were wrong there, Dad," Carole said.

"Well, look, honey. I made a mistake and I'm sorry about it, but let's make the best of it. Now let me see your pretty new dress, won't you? It's all Lynne talked about when you two got back. It must be something!"

Carole could be stubborn, but she could also tell when she had lost a fight. If she was going to have to go to the dance at the Officers' Club, she would at least make the best of it. Maybe it would be fun after all. She nodded to her father and went upstairs to change into her new white cotton lace dress. She and Lynne had bought a pair of white sandals to go with the dress, so she slipped them on as well. Then, as an afterthought, Carole used a red ribbon to hold her hair back. She scampered downstairs for the fashion show.

Her father had settled onto his favorite television-watching couch, preparing for *The D.I.*, which would go on in fifteen minutes.

"Like it, Dad?" she asked, stepping into the living room.

The colonel looked over his shoulder at Carole and then swung his feet back off the couch and onto the floor so he could get a better look.

"Oh, my!" he said, grinning broadly. "You *are* beautiful."

Carole blushed. "Thanks, Dad," she said, twirling around to show him how nicely the skirt flared.

He smiled appreciatively. "I'm so proud of you, honey," the colonel said. "I just wish your mother could see what a beautiful woman you're becoming. She'd be proud, too."

"Thanks, Dad," Carole said, knowing that she had done the right thing by agreeing to go to the dance. Even if she didn't want to do it, it would mean an awful lot to her father. It wasn't until much later that Carole began to wonder: What was so special about this dance?

And who was she going to invite to go with her?

"LISA, YOU SHOULD sit back a little in the saddle, especially when you're trotting," Carole advised her friend. "Just try sitting up straighter and you'll find you balance better."

Lisa straightened her back and immediately improved her seat. "It seems so simple when you say it. The only problem is remembering it when you're not here to remind me!" Lisa said.

"Oh, you'll remember in time," Stevie said. "You just get so used to it that it becomes natural."

"I can't wait for that moment!" Lisa said.

Carole smiled. Lisa had been working very hard at her riding since she had started only a few months before. If only she knew how long it took most riders to be as good as Lisa had already become!

"Patience," Carole advised. "You're doing great!"

The three girls were out on a trail ride by themselves on Monday morning. Stevie had talked Max into letting them take a picnic into the woods. They had all hopped onto their horses and headed for the cover of the forest before he could change his mind.

It was a beautiful summer day. The sky was a deep blue with a few wisps of white clouds for contrast. It wasn't too hot, for once, and it wasn't muggy at all. In the forest, the sunshine made a dappled shadow pattern, which changed constantly when the soft breeze swished through the leaves.

Carole brought Diablo to a walk and the others followed. Horseback riding was something Carole could count on. Often it seemed to her that the world was confusing and unreliable. Her mother's death had proved that, and now Scott's unwanted attention and her father's insistence about the dance next weekend seemed to confirm her suspicions that she couldn't control events. But whenever Carole was riding, she was in charge of the world, or at least the part of the world that mattered to her. Her body moved in perfect rhythm with Diablo's walk. She felt the power of the animal underneath her and she knew that power was hers. It was a very comforting feeling.

Ahead, the trail split in two. One way led to an open pasture. The other, to the right, followed Willow

Creek, after which their town was named. Carole gently turned Diablo to the right. Her friends followed on their horses. Carole was in charge. And she liked it that way.

"I thought we'd stop at the place where the creek gets so wide," she said. "We can have our picnic and water the horses—"

"And wade," Stevie finished the sentence for her.

Carole nodded. The creek's cool water would feel good on her feet and ankles, which had been encased in hot leather boots all morning. "Let's trot for a while, then we can canter where the trail crosses the meadow and walk until we get to the creek." She signaled Diablo to trot, and once he had a nice collected trot she began posting, rising and sitting with the rhythm of his gait.

When the path widened, Stevie drew Comanche up next to Diablo and Carole. "So where was the dramatic rescue with Scott?" she asked. "It was on this trail, wasn't it?"

Carole nodded. "The thunder began when we got to the big old oak at the curve next to the meadow," she explained. "Right up there." She pointed up ahead about thirty yards. "Patch took off down the hill away from the trail. Scott was hopeless, too."

"If you want my opinion, he's still hopeless—I mean hopelessly in love with you!"

"I think you're right—and I can assure you that one day of perfectly awful stable chores hasn't done anything to change his mind. Some bright idea. All it got me was a bunch of blisters!"

"Sorry about that," Stevie said. "I tried!"

"I'm sure," Carole teased. "Next time, you do the mucking out, okay?" She laughed. "I'm just joking. Those stables needed cleaning anyway, and at least I got some help doing it."

"So it wasn't such a bad idea after all."

"Well . . . anyway, it didn't accomplish what we wanted to accomplish."

"Relax, Carole," Stevie said soothingly. "I've got a few tricks up my sleeve yet."

"That's what I was afraid of!" Carole said, laughing. One thing she knew she could *always* count on was that Stevie would have big ideas. And no matter whether they worked or not, it was one of the reasons Carole like her so much.

They passed the point where Patch had bolted. Soon after that, the trail crossed the meadow. The three girls sat down in their saddles while their horses continued trotting and then touched the horses behind their girths on one side. Soon the horses were cantering, the wonderful rocking-horse gait. Carole sat deeply into the saddle, moving forward and back with the horse's motions. She loved almost everything about riding, but it was hard to think of anything more fun than cantering gently across an open field on a graceful horse like Diablo, with the bright, warm sunshine beaming down from above. The tangy smell of the hay in the meadow blended perfectly with the rich smell of horses and leather. Carole was content.

When they had crossed the meadow, the girls drew the horses to a walk so they could cool down for the last ten minutes of the ride until they reached the creek.

"Okay, lunchtime!" Carole announced, dismounting. "For the horses, of course."

The Saddle Club knew the horses came first. There would be plenty of time for the girls to eat and relax once they had tended to the horses.

The girls loosened the girths and put halters over the horses' bridles so they could snap lead ropes onto them. In spite of cowboys who tied their horses' reins to hitching posts in movies, The Saddle Club knew that it was very bad for the horse, and the reins, to use them that way. The girls led the horses to the creek and let them have a cooling drink, but not too much. A whole lot of cold water in a horse's stomach on a hot day could lead to digestive problems very quickly. When the horses were refreshed, the girls tied them up where they could reach sweet, fresh grass for snacking. After the horses were tended, it was the girls' turn to rest.

"Last one in is a rotten egg," Stevie said, removing her boots. She rolled up her pants legs and then sat on a big flat rock that bordered the creek. She dangled her feet in the water. "Heaven," she announced. Carole and Lisa quickly followed suit.

Lisa hauled out the sandwiches and juice and passed them around.

"It's so nice out today that even a peanut-butter sandwich tastes like a feast."

"Well, today's sure a lot better than Saturday," Carole told her friends.

"What happened Saturday?" Lisa asked her. She and Stevie had been so involved in their own disastrous day as models that it hadn't even occurred to her to wonder what Carole had been up to.

"I went shopping for a dress," Carole said, as if that were an explanation.

"I *love* shopping," Stevie said.

"Me, too," Lisa piped in. "Unless my mother's with me. Then what she does is to practically lock me in a dressing room and bombard me with the most hideous dresses."

"Tell me about it," Carole said, rolling her eyes.

"Oh, there was this one that she kept on about once. It made me look about eight years old!"

"Did it have tons of little roses?" Carole asked.

"No. Balloons," Lisa told her.

77

Carole gulped. Maybe Lynne wasn's so bad after all!

"What was so awful about shopping Saturday?" Stevie asked.

"Well, I had to go with Lynne Blessing. You know, the woman my dad's been dating? She tries to be nice to me, but she just doesn't get it. It was just exactly what Lisa described. It was like she was trying to make me into something I'm not. I try to be nice to her, because she's Dad's friend, but it gets hard sometimes."

"Sounds like a mother," Lisa remarked. "She's always trying to make me into something I'm not, too."

"I had a mother," Carole said. "She was terrific. I even used to like to go shopping with her. It wasn't at all the way it was with Lynne." Carole described Lynne's actions, her overbearing enthusiasm about Carole's outfit, and the dance Carole had been "persuaded" to attend.

While Carole completed her description of the day, Stevie leaned back on the rock, resting her head on the saddlebags, which had held their picnic. Her feet were still dangling in the cool water. She kicked gently, stirring up the creek and sprinkling her friends with occasional drops of water. It was her way of thinking.

"I think Lisa said the key word," Stevie said after a few minutes of thought. "And the key word is 'mother.'"

"What are you driving at?" Carole asked.

"It sounds an awful lot to me like Lynne is trying to be somebody's mother, specificially *your* mother—make that your *step*mother."

"You think she wants to *marry* Dad?" Carole yelped.

"Yes, I do," Stevie said positively. "Especially from the part about the dinner dance and the cozy table for four."

Carole eyed her friends. They looked at her expectantly. "When you put it that way, the symptoms are clear, aren't they?" Carole asked. Her friends nodded. "Just great," she said with a sigh.

"I thought you *wanted* your dad to go out on dates," Lisa said.

Carole looked thoughtfully at the water as it rolled slowly past her feet, constantly changing and swirling around her. "I did. I mean, I do. He should have fun," she said sensibly. "I even thought it would be nice for him to have a *serious* girlfriend. The problem isn't him having a girlfriend. The problem is the girlfriend being Lynne. She's okay, in some ways, but I can't see spending all of my teenage years trying to deal with her."

The girls were all silent for a while. The only sounds were the contented munching of the horses and the girls' feet splashing idly in the creek.

"Looks to me like we've got another problem,"

Stevie announced. "And we're going to have to solve it."

One of the things Carole liked about her friends was that when *she* had a problem, they always wanted to help her solve it. When you had friends like The Saddle Club, you were never alone.

"MY TURN TO lead," Stevie announced, mounting Comanche. The horses were rested, the picnic was finished, and it was time to return to Pine Hollow.

"Okay, but wait a second," Lisa said. "I've got to get my boots back on. It's not easy in this heat!" Stevie favored cowboy boots for riding, and those were always easy to slip into. Carole usually wore low jodhpur boots. But Lisa's boots had been selected by her fashion-conscious mother and they were high black riding boots. They were designed to be pulled on with special hooks.

Carole stood behind Lisa and helped her tug until the boots finally came up over her calves. "Remind me to buy my own riding clothes next time," Lisa said dully. "I'd much rather have low boots than these things."

"They really ought to have built-in hooks," Carole remarked as she mounted Diablo. Then she and Stevie waited until Lisa was ready to go. Soon Lisa, too, was mounted. Before they left the picnic site, the girls carefully scanned the area to be sure they hadn't left any garbage behind. It was an unbreakable Pine Hollow rule that no litter would ever be left behind. Since today's picnic was a special privilege, they wanted to make especially certain that they were observing the rules. Satisfied that the area was the same as they had found it, they followed Stevie along the trail.

Stevie, their fearless leader, chattered continuously as they walked their horses through the glen.

"Okay, now the first thing you do with Lynne is to turn her off your dad. You can talk about all his other girlfriends."

"You don't know Lynne," Carole said. "I think that's the sort of thing she'd take as a challenge. I mean, we're talking about one determined woman. You should have seen her at the mall with me. As long as she thinks Dad's interested in her in the slightest, she'll hold onto him like a tick to a horse's belly!"

"What a disgusting thought!" Stevie said, turning around in the saddle to make a face at Carole. Carole shrugged.

"Okay, then, instead of making him a challenge for Lynne, how about you tell her *all* about him—you know, his deepest secrets and nastiest habits?" Lisa suggested.

Carole furrowed her brows. "Trouble with that is that I think he's just fine. How can I make him sound bad to her? He doesn't really have many bad habits, anyway."

"What about all those awful old jokes he's always telling Stevie?" Lisa asked.

"What's the matter with old jokes?" Stevie demanded.

"All right, all right. But not everybody likes them, and not everybody likes ancient movies, either," Lisa said.

"I do," Carole said. "You should have seen the one we watched the other night—*The D.I.* This guy, supposedly a Marine Corps drill instructor, gets all these guys digging up sand, looking for a tsetse fly one of them slapped when he wasn't supposed to. Another bunch is digging a huge trench that's supposed to be a grave for the tsetse fly . . ." Carole's shoulders began shaking with laughter. Soon she was laughing so hard that she couldn't go on with the explanation of what was apparently hilariously funny to her.

Lisa and Stevie exchanged looks. "Maybe it's one of those things where you just had to be there," Lisa suggested tentatively.

"Whatever it is, I can assure you that Carole loves

old movies just as much as her dad does and there's *no way* she'd ever convince Lynne it's a bad habit."

"You got that right," Lisa agreed.

They continued riding along the trail quietly. The silence of the forest was broken occasionally by snorts from Carole as she recalled other tidbits from the movie she had watched with her father.

"Oh, and there was the time the guy—"

"Spare us!" Stevie cried, cutting her off. "Lisa and I will rent it one night and see it on our own. Okay?"

"Okay," Carole agreed, still giggling to herself.

"Now, back to the business of de-Lynning your father. How about you tell her how much fun it is to live with somebody in the Marine Corps—like how you have to move all the time, and how your dad has to make long trips and you can't go along with him? Remember the four months he spent in Kodiak, Alaska?"

Carole shook her head. "For one thing, Dad's senior enough now that he's not likely to get moved unless he wants it. And, for another, if he were to go off to Alaska for four months again, Lynne would absolutely *insist* on staying with me and taking care of me. I don't even want to mention the possibility. She'd move into our house in the blink of an eye!"

"You could stay with me," Stevie said.

"Or me!" Lisa added. "We'd be glad to have you. We

even have two extra bedrooms. No problem. I'm pretty sure my mom would agree."

"Well, I *know* my mom would. Since there are already four kids in the house, she probably wouldn't even notice," Stevie said. "It would be great—"

Carole grinned. "Listen, I appreciate the invitations, you guys, but that's not exactly the problem we have to solve right now. The problem is *Lynne,* not me."

"Oh, yeah," Stevie said. She had gotten distracted by the exciting idea of having Carole live with her for a few months.

"Why don't you make up some bad habits for your dad?" Lisa suggested.

"Like collecting beer cans, matchbook covers, bugs, stuff like that?" Carole asked suspicously. "This is beginning to sound an awful lot like the bright ideas you had about Scott, which didn't work. Maybe I should get good old Lynne to muck out some stalls!"

"Now *there's* an idea," Stevie said. "Only problem is that it would be sure to confuse Max even more. He's *still* going around mumbling about the 'wonder boy' who cleaned out the stalls the other day—"

"Uh, I hate to interrupt your brainstorm, Stevie," Lisa said, "but where are we?"

"We're on the—why?"

"Just wondering. Are we lost?"

"How can we be lost if we're here?" Stevie countered.

"Where's 'here'?" Lisa asked persistently.

Stevie glanced at the woods around her. "Carole, you tell her," Stevie said.

Carole looked around for familiar landmarks, but there weren't any. "You're the trail leader," she said. "You get to tell her—and me too," she added pointedly.

"Well, we're almost to, uh, and we can't be far from, the, ah, you know."

"Does this mean we're lost?" Lisa asked, turning to Carole.

"Sounds like it to me," she said, laughing at Stevie's antics. But she wasn't really worried. She knew they couldn't have ridden too far; they would come across a familiar landmark sooner or later. "Aren't you glad Stevie's in the lead?"

"Yeah, it reminds me of my first trail ride. Remember her 'shortcut'?"

It would have been hard for anyone, but especially Lisa, to forget Stevie's shortcut that day. Stevie had taken them through a field inhabited by a very unhappy bull. The three girls had ended up jumping over a big fence—a difficult feat for an experienced rider, an astonishing feat for Lisa, who had only been riding for a few weeks at the time.

"Hey, there's a road up ahead," Stevie said. "At the least, we can follow the road signs—"

"To Timbuktu!" Lisa finished her sentence for her. Riding with Stevie, it seemed, was always an adventure.

Rather sheepishly, Stevie led the way onto the two-lane road. "Which way, fearless leader?" Carole asked.

"I'm not sure," Stevie told her. "But either left or right, I think."

"What thinking!" Lisa teased.

"All right, my mind's made up," Stevie said. "We're turning left." With that, she turned Comanche to the left and got him walking along the edge of the road. Smiling at each other, Lisa and Carole followed her.

It was a little annoying to be lost, but the girls knew perfectly well that they couldn't be *too* far from the stable and they would get back there before long.

A few cars whizzed past them as they continued along the road, alternately walking and trotting. Since Stevie was supposedly leading them, it was up to her to stop somebody to ask where they were.

Another car came up from behind them but it didn't pass. It just kept going slower and slower.

Then a familiar voice spoke from the car's window.

"Carole?" Carole turned to see Scott, waving at her. "What are you doing here?" he asked.

"We're having a sort of off-trail ride," she explained.

"Max told me you guys were on a trail ride, but I thought you'd be heading home by now."

"We are," she said.

"But you're going *away* from the stable," he said.

"We are?" she responded, only a little bit surprised.

"Sure, Pine Hollow's back that way. We just came from there," he said to her. "We took a left off of Attington Way into this old road."

So *that's* where they were! That meant this was the old country road that skirted the forest land outside the town of Willow Creek. It led to a camping area. Since people who lived in Willow Creek didn't usually camp there, it wasn't familiar to The Saddle Club. They were really lucky that the Babcocks had come along that route. It might have been another hour until they got to the camping area and realized their mistake!

"Yo! Lisa, Stevie!" Carole called. When her friends turned around to see why she was calling, she waved them over to Scott's father's car. "We've certainly enjoyed this scenic tour, Stevie," Carole teased as they joined her. "But I think it's time to head back to Pine Hollow now, don't you?" She really didn't want Scott to know they had been lost, but she wasn't fooling him at all.

"Does that mean I've saved *your* life now?" he asked.

She smiled at him. "I suppose so," she admitted. " I guess that makes us even."

"Right," he said, grinning back at her. "Anyway, I'm glad I could help you out."

"So am I," she admitted. "We've got to get the horses back now, though. See you around."

"Sure," he said, waving as she walked off. Then, before his father had a chance to start the car moving, Scott turned in his seat and hung out of the window of the passenger side of the car. "In fact, how about Saturday? Could I see you then? Want to go out?"

Scott caught her by surprise. She glanced quickly at her friends, who were unsuccessfully suppressing grins.

"Uh, w-well . . ." she stammered. Then she realized that this might be a blessing in disguise. "Hey, there's a dance at the Officers' Club I have to go to. Want to go to that?"

"Do I ever!" he responded.

What *was* she doing? she asked herself.

"Okay, then, come to my house about six-thirty, okay?"

"I'll be there," he said, drawing himself back into the car. His father started driving away. Carole watched as the car suddenly screeched to a halt and backed up to where she was still halted on Diablo.

Scott's embarrassed face emerged from the window once again. "Uh—where do you live?" he asked.

She told him, and the Babcocks drove off for the final time.

"You really know how to shake off a guy, don't you?" Stevie asked in mock admiration.

"Well, I've got to have a date for this dumb dance, so it might as well be dumb old Scott," Carole retorted. "Besides, maybe it'll be easier to kill two birds with one stone, don't you think?"

"No," Lisa and Stevie said at the same time.

CAROLE GAZED AT herself in the mirror of her bedroom on Saturday evening. All week long, it had seemed as if she couldn't make up her mind whether she wanted Saturday to come or stay away. Now, here it was Saturday and she *still* couldn't make up her mind. Stevie and Lisa were having a sleepover at Stevie's house. She wished she were there.

Then she glanced over at her bed, where her new white dress was laid out. She smiled. It *was* pretty. She really liked the neckline and the simple eyelet lace. She slipped the dress on over her head and zipped it up. She was trying to reach the hook to fasten it when she passed her mirror again. Studying her reflection, she decided she was glad it was Saturday after all.

Carole heard the Babcocks' car pull into her driveway. She glanced out the window and watched Scott emerge. He gazed up at the house uncertainly and then approached the front door. Carole heard the doorbell ring. Her father answered it. A few seconds later, Dr. Babcock drove away.

There was a knock at her door. "Honey, I know you saw the car so you know Scott's here. I'm pretending you don't, though, so I have a chance to come see you and see if you need any help. Any hooks that need hooking?"

Carole smiled to herself. Her father was just about the neatest guy in the world. No wonder Lynne couldn't leave him alone. "Yes," she said. "There *is* one. " Her father came into her room and helped her with the hook at the top of her zipper. When it was all done, she wrapped Lynne's shawl around her shoulders and spun around for effect.

"Well?" she asked.

"Well, what?"

"Well, how do you like it?"

"I love it—except for the shawl. Where did that come from?"

Carole giggled. "Lynne loaned it to me. She said it 'accents the outfit perfectly.' I think I have to wear it, Dad," Carole said.

"Oh."

"It's time now, huh?"

He nodded, then offered Carole his arm.

"ARE THE MARSHMALLOWS melted yet?" Stevie asked Lisa. The girls had shooed everybody out of the kitchen right after supper so they could make a special dessert for themselves.

"What *are* you making?" Stevie's twin brother, Alex, asked from outside the kitchen door. "It smells great. Can I have some? Please?"

Stevie turned to the closed door and put her hands on her hips. "None of your business. No. And no." She turned back to Lisa. "You are *so* lucky, having only one brother. You don't know."

"Maybe," Lisa said noncommittally. "But there's always so much going on here. It's exciting. Fun! My family is just plain boring."

"Well, I'll give you that," Stevie agreed. "Living here isn't boring. Crazy, maybe. Certainly not boring."

Lisa looked down at the pot of goo she was stirring. "Guess what? I think it's *time.*"

Stevie smacked her lips. "Okay, then it's time to mix." At Lisa's signal, Stevie poured the Rice Krispies into the melted marshmallows and Lisa began stirring. When the mixture had gotten wonderfully gooey and impossibly sticky, they began pressing it into the square glass baking dish, using butter-covered utensils. That didn't mean that the sweet mess didn't get stuck on them anyway, but it didn't matter. That simply gave them an opportunity to lick it off, getting a taste of what was to come.

"Not a bite. My brothers won't get even the tiniest little taste," Stevie vowed. "You and I'll hoard it for ourselves."

They were getting down to the serious business of contemplating how delicious the concoction was going to be when a car pulled up in the Lakes' driveway and the doorbell rang.

A few seconds later, Alex burst into the kitchen, uninvited. "Stevie, it's that photographer lady—Jackie something. She says she's got some pictures to show you. She seems all excited."

At the very mention of the photographer's name, the girls' glamorized images of the Life of a Model came rushing back into their minds. "Maybe the pictures of us were *really* good," Stevie said. "Maybe—"

"Maybe we actually do have a chance, you mean?" Lisa asked.

"Maybe," Stevie said. "So let's find out!"

They washed their hands quickly and dropped their cooking utensils in the sink. Then they covered their snack with waxed paper and headed for the living room, where Jackie was waiting for them.

"I was in the neighborhood and I just couldn't wait to show you, girls! What luck that you're both here together! The pictures are wonderful!"

"They are?" Lisa asked.

"Do we look good?" Stevie piped up.

"You look fabulous!" Jackie exclaimed. "Come see!"

She opened up the portfolio she was carrying and began spreading photographs all over the coffee table and the sofa. "Look, here are the boots," Jackie said, showing them a perfectly nice photograph of a pair of high boots and then one of some jodhpur boots. "Isn't the composition terrific?"

"Uh, sure," Stevie said. "Really nice."

"And here's the horse blanket." The girls looked to see Comanche standing perfectly still, modeling a navy-blue horse blanket. There was no sign of Lisa, who had been hiding on the horse's far side, nor of Stevie, who had been off to the side, getting Comanche's attention.

"And look at these pictures of the bridles! Look, there you are, Lisa."

Lisa's ears perked up when she heard her name. This was the moment she had been waiting for. She leaned over the table, eager to see herself—and she did. At least, she saw her hands. They were holding the reins of the bridle, but her grip was improper.

"You can't use that picture!" Lisa said in dismay. "I'm not holding the reins right." Lisa wanted to kick herself. Her big chance, and she'd blown it!

"You're not?" Jackie asked in surprise. The girls both

told her it was true. Any rider would recognize that the reins had to go between her third and fourth fingers. In this photograph, she was just grasping them. "Oh, don't worry," Jackie said. "I can crop that part out. What's important is the bridle."

Lisa sighed. So much for her career as a model.

"There's your knee, Stevie," Jackie said. The girls looked. It was a photograph of a saddlebag. There was a knee visible. The knee *could* have been Stevie's.

"Look how nicely *this* saddle came out," Jackie said, showing them one of the saddles perched on the wooden saddle rack. Lisa thought she saw a shadow on the far side of the saddle that might have been her hand as she kept the equipment from toppling. She pointed it out to Jackie.

"Oh, I think you're right," the photographer said. "I can airbrush that shadow out. No problem."

Lisa was going to end up on the cutting-room floor!

"You girls were really wonderful," Jackie told them. "I really appreciated your help. Being a photographer's aide isn't easy and you just pitched in and helped me in every possible way. I wanted you to see these right away because they came out so nicely. I'm just certain the catalog people are going to want me to do more work for them and I promise I'll call you to help me as soon as I hear from them."

"We can't wait," Stevie said, very unenthusiastically. But she managed a smile. So did Lisa.

"Well, it's settled, then. In the meantime, I've brought you each an envelope with your pay in it. I wish it could have been twice as much!"

"So do we!" Stevie said brightly. Jackie laughed.

A few minutes later, she had left and the girls were alone with their envelopes and their broken dreams.

"Fifty dollars *seemed* like all the money in the world," Stevie said wistfully. "Now, for some reason, it doesn't seem like so much."

"It isn't, really," Lisa said. "It just seemed that way when we thought the work was going to be easy. We would have agreed to model for her whether we were getting paid or not."

"So what are we going to do with our money?" Stevie asked. "Maybe we can spend it on something we can do together with Carole."

"I don't know, but it ought to be something special. Something that might make up for the fact that we haven't even told Carole about the pictures."

"That's going to be hard to do. Personally, I feel rotten about keeping this whole thing a secret from her."

"So do I," Lisa agreed. She sat on the sofa in Stevie's living room, staring unhappily at the floor. "Maybe the only way to make it up to Carole is to share the money with her."

Stevie's eyes lit up. "That's a wonderful idea," she

said. "You know, she's been saving every penny she can for her airfare to visit Kate Devine. I bet this money would put her over the top!"

"Wouldn't that be terrific?" Lisa agreed. "It's a deal, then. Giving Carole the money will be a lot more fun than modeling ever was!"

"Who ever said modeling was fun?" Stevie countered.

"Oh, I don't know. I had a lot of fun in my dreams."

"Me, too." Stevie shrugged. Then she turned to the kitchen. "What was that noise?" she asked suspiciously.

Lisa's face fell. "Oh, no," she said.

The two girls dashed for the kitchen doorway. When they got there, they saw Stevie's three brothers seated at the kitchen table, happily finishing off their Rice Krispies Treats.

Chad, Stevie's fourteen-year-old brother, was the first to speak. "You'll be pleased to know that you two made the most delicious treat for us! We loved it and we thank you *very* much!" His eyes twinkled.

Stevie and Lisa were so astonished by his announcement that they could only laugh.

"At least we did something right," Lisa said.

"Maybe we can have a career as pastry chefs," Stevie

chimed in, secretly pleased at how much her brothers had liked their cooking.

"Can I have some more?" Michael, the youngest, asked.

Stevie shrugged. "Sure, why not? Come on, Lisa, let's cook up another batch."

Lisa happily reached for the marshmallow bag and poured from it into a large measuring cup.

"I JUST CAN'T wait for the dance contest," Lynne bubbled, her eyes sparkling as she gazed at the colonel.

"What dance contest?" Carole asked suspiciously. Since Lynne seemed so good at planning everybody's life, Carole was more than a little bit concerned that she might find herself in a dance contest.

The four of them—Carole, Scott Babcock, Lynne, and Carole's father—were seated at a table in the ballroom of the Officers' Club at the Marine Corps base at Quantico. Usually, this was the dining room, but tonight it had been transformed. Toys for Tots was a project sponsored by the Marine Corps Reserve, in which the Corps raised money to buy toys for children whose parents couldn't afford presents for them. The ballroom was decorated like a child's paradise. The ceiling was hidden by fluffy pink and blue cotton puff clouds. Suspended beneath the clouds were wonderfully inviting toys: stuffed animals, trucks, dolls, baseball gloves. The walls around the room were covered with posters advertising toys and books for children. It was impossible to forget the purpose of the dance. Carole hoped they raised a lot of money for the very worthy cause. But just then she was more concerned about a certain dance contest.

"So what about the dance contest?" Carole asked dubiously.

"It's a twist contest!"

"I can't do the twist!" Carole protested.

"Of course not!" Lynne said. "It's your dad and I who are going to do the twist. He and I are couple number, uh, eighteen. But not for long. Practically as soon as the contest starts we'll be *couple number one!* Mitch is the greatest dancer—especially with these old-time dances!"

"What do you mean, 'old-time dances'?" he teased, pretending his feelings had been hurt. "I'm not so old." He winked at Carole.

Carole smiled at her father. He did love old songs and dances, as well as movies—not to mention jokes. And apparently he was a good dancer, too. The gyrations involved looked rather strange to Carole, but everybody said he was good, so maybe he was.

"So what's the prize for couple number one?" Carole asked Lynne.

"*That's* the good news, honey," Lynne said. Carole cringed a little bit. She hated it when Lynne called her "honey." Lynne continued excitedly. "First prize is a pair of round-trip airplane tickets, anywhere in the U.S. Can you believe it? Won't it be wonderful?"

That was odd. What would Lynne and her father do with airplane tickets? Her father did so much traveling for his job that he really didn't enjoy traveling. And he would never go on a trip with Lynne and leave Carole alone. *Would he?*

"What's the matter, Carole?" Scott asked.

She hadn't realized she was making a face. She turned to him. "Nothing, I was just thinking," she explained.

"You looked like you were thinking bad thoughts," he persisted.

He was nice about the way he said it, but it felt like he was prying and Carole didn't want to talk with Scott about Lynne. After all, part of her plan tonight was to try to break up *two* romances. So far, the plan didn't seem to be working at all.

"Want to dance?" he asked.

"Sure," she agreed, standing up from the table. It would be nice to be away from Lynne's gushing for a few minutes at least.

The band was playing a slow dance and Scott seemed unsure of what to do. He glanced around at the other couples.

"Never had to go to dancing school?" Carole asked.

He laughed sheepishly. "I always talked my mother out of it," he explained.

"It was my *father* who insisted," Carole told him. "Here, let me show you what to do." She put his right hand on her back and held his left with her right. "Now, we make little squares on the floor. It's called a box step. Step slide, step slide. I go backward. You go forward. Then vice versa. Got it? Hey, not bad," she commented as Scott more or less successfully followed her instructions.

Within a few minutes, they were dancing easily with each other. She only stepped on Scott's foot once. He only stepped on hers five times.

"You can't possibly be enjoying this," he said, observing her grimace as he landed particularly hard on her toe.

"Oh, it's fine. And besides, it's better to be here than to be there," she said, nodding at the table where her father and Lynne were talking with their heads close together.

"You don't like her?" Scott asked.

"She's okay, I guess, but she keeps trying to manage my life."

"It's hard to imagine somebody pushing *you* around," he said. Then Scott began watching his feet. Carole knew he was being careful not to step on her toes again. While he concentrated on that, she could think about her father and Lynne some more.

So far, the evening had gone well enough. Carole was comfortable at the Officers' Club. There were plenty of people she and her father knew. The colonel had introduced Lynne to a lot of the other officers and their wives. Carole and Scott had spent some time with some of the other "military brats" she had known when they had lived on the base and Carole had gone to school there.

The decorations were special. The food was pretty good. The music was nice. Scott was okay. So why wasn't she having any fun? It could be summed up in one word: Lynne.

Two round-trip tickets to anyplace in the country. If it were just Carole and her father, she knew what she would want to do. She would want the two of them to visit her new friend Kate Devine and her parents at their dude ranch. But Lynne and her dad?

Suddenly, Carole had an awful thought. "Oh, no!" she said.

"Did I step on something?" Scott asked.

"No. It's just that . . ." She couldn't say it. She couldn't say the word to Scott. Because the word that was in her mind was "honeymoon." If two people were going to get married, the one thing they would want, more than anything else, would be two round-trip airplane tickets to anywhere in the country. They wouldn't want three. Because only two people would go.

*That* would explain why Lynne and her dad were so eager to win the prize in the dance contest. That would explain why they were talking to each other with their heads *so* close. And that would explain why Carole had such a bad feeling about the evening!

"Carole, what's the matter?" Scott asked, suddenly very worried. "Why are you crying?"

Carole was so upset that she hadn't even realized that she *was* crying.

"I'm not crying," she said, trying to fake it, but the fact was that the tears were streaming down her face and she couldn't fool anybody. "I've got to go to the ladies' room," she said, and then fled from the dance floor. She *had* to be alone!

All the bright colors of the ballroom merged into one gigantic rainbow of confusion. The noise of the crowd and the strains of the music blended into a muddle of discordant sounds. Carole didn't see any faces, hear any greetings, or even feel the floor under her feet. The only thing she was aware of was one word: honeymoon. It had to be the answer. Lynne and her father were planning to be married and they were going to go on a trip together afterward.

Carole realized then, as she had never realized before, that she didn't want to share her father with anybody; and she especially couldn't stand the idea of sharing him with Lynne!

The tears were pouring out of her eyes so fast that she could barely see as she wound her way through the room. Without even realizing she was doing it, Carole ran smack into a tray caddy, and before she knew what had happened she was on the floor. Her right ankle had caught in the folded-up legs of the caddy, and within seconds it swelled to twice its normal size.

Carole's tears of anguish and fear were suddenly replaced by tears of pain. Her ankle *hurt*. The first person to reach her was Scott.

He sat down on the floor by her side, taking her hand.

"Are you okay?" he asked.

"I hurt my ankle," she told him.

He looked at it, examining it carefully. "You sure did that," he agreed. He turned to the waiter who was standing there and asked him to get some ice, wrapped in a wet cloth napkin. When the waiter returned, Scott applied the ice pack to Carole's ankle, and the pain began to subside.

When Carole's father arrived on the scene, he and

Scott helped Carole stand up and hobble back to their table. Scott grabbed a fifth chair, giving Carole something to prop her foot up on, and they soon surrounded her ankle with additional supplies of ice.

"I've got so much ice here, I should go skating instead of dancing?" Carole said, trying to make light of the situation.

"I don't think you're doing to be doing either for a couple of days," her father said wisely.

"I twisted my ankle like that once," Lynne said. "It took *weeks* for it to heal."

Carole groaned. "My ankle's so swollen, I couldn't even get my boots on to ride. You can't mean it that it's going to last for weeks."

"Probably not, hon," her father said. "Scott was pretty smart getting the ice for it so fast, though. That will reduce the swelling. Thanks, Scott," the colonel said to him.

"Yeah, thank you," Carole echoed.

"Oh, it was nothing," Scott said. "I was just the first one there. You would have done the same thing," he added to her father.

It was true, Carole thought. Scott was there because her father was too busy with Lynne to notice that she had fallen down until a big crowd had gathered around her. She had almost forgotten how upset she had been about Lynne and her father until Scott reminded her.

She still wanted to leave—and the sooner the better.

"Dad, I think I'd better go home," she said.

"Okay, Carole, I'll drive you." He stood up to go.

"Mitch! You can't *do* that!" Lynne said. "Remember the dance contest? It's going to kick off in about a half hour. There's no way you'll get back in time. And it's so important."

The colonel looked at Lynne, then he looked at his daughter. "She's right, Carole. Can you wait until the contest is over?"

Carole was about to tell her father that there was no way she could wait. This was the opportunity she had hoped for—a surefire way to upset the plans for a honeymoon trip!

"No problem, sir," Scott interrupted. "The friends we're staying with live just outside the base. I can call my dad. He'll pick us up and we'll see Carole home. You and Ms. Blessing can stay for the dance contest. I saw you out there on the floor earlier. You guys are a shoo-in to win—you can't miss it!"

Colonel Hanson protested for a moment, but Lynne quickly talked him into accepting Scott's offer, particularly when Scott reminded him that his father was a doctor and would take a look at Carole's ankle to be sure it wasn't more serious than they thought.

Carole sat glumly while the talking was going on.

She didn't like any of it, but nobody was asking for *her* opinion.

Before the dance contest began, she found herself being settled in the back seat of the Babcocks' station wagon, to be taken home by Scott and Dr. Babcock. *Oh, sure,* she thought, her father waving as they pulled out of the parking lot. *Your dumb old dance with Lynne is more important than your own daughter!*

The good news was that the doctor thought her ankle was just mildly sprained and she would be back up and around by Tuesday. The bad news? It seemed to Carole that *everything* else was bad news.

ON MONDAY MORNING, Stevie stood in the aisle of the stable with her hands on her hips. It was chore time and she was in charge of getting fresh water for the horses. It wasn't a bad chore, as chores went, but the buckets could get very heavy. Usually, Carole would help her, but Carole was staying home to take care of her ankle and, Stevie suspected, to mope. Saturday night had not gone at all the way Carole had wanted. Carole was convinced her father was going to marry Lynne, and Scott had been so nice to her that she hadn't made any headway at all in discouraging him.

Stevie felt bad about all of Carole's troubles, but it wasn't helping her get water for the horses. She sighed audibly. Then she blinked her eyes. Could she be seeing things? Or was it a dream come true?

"Scott? Is that you?" she asked. It was hard to see in the dim light of the stables, particularly with the bright morning light streaming in from behind the tall figure who had just entered the stable.

"Yes, it's me," he answered. "Is Carole here this morning?"

"No, she's not coming today. I talked to her before breakfast, though. She said her ankle was better, but she's not coming in until tomorrow. She doesn't want to push it."

"I was just passing by," he said casually, but Stevie didn't believe it for a second. The place Scott was staying was *miles* away from Pine Hollow. Nobody just passed by from that far away. "I didn't talk to her yesterday so I thought maybe her ankle would be better by now. I'll stop by again tomorrow." He turned to leave, but Stevie didn't want him to go. Stevie's mind was always quick, but two things could make it particularly quick. One was when she *might* be able to find somebody to do chores for her and the other was when she could do a favor for a friend. She had the sneaking suspicion she could accomplish both at the same time if she could get Scott to stay.

"Gee, Scott, as long as you're here, could you give

me a hand with something?" she asked. Then she held her breath.

"Mucking out stables?" he asked with a smile.

Stevie stifled a giggle. "Oh, no. It's just carrying heavy buckets."

"No problem," he said.

That's what *he* thought!

Each horse had a large blue plastic bucket suspended from a hook in his stall. They all needed fresh water in the morning and that meant hefting the empty buckets to the faucet, rinsing them out with cold running water, and then lugging the full buckets back to the stalls. The full buckets were very heavy. But luckily, Scott was very strong.

As good as he had been with mucking out stables, he was even better with the heavy buckets. Soon, Stevie found herself trotting along beside him as he took over the task. With her hands free, she was able to concentrate solely on the job she had put to herself— breaking up Scott's romance with Carole.

"You have a good time on Saturday?" she asked innocently. She needed some way to get to talking about Carole so she could give Scott the impression that Carole wasn't his kind of girl at all. Her mind was racing.

"Sure did," he said. "Carole's a terrific dancer."

"Really? I would have thought she spent too much time with her stamp collection to learn to dance."

Stevie thought stamp collections were too dull for words. She hoped Scott agreed. But he didn't seem to notice.

"And she was wearing the prettiest dress," Scott remarked.

"Oh, sure. She makes all her own clothes," Stevie told him. She had once met a very drippy girl who sewed a lot. "Most of them come out okay. Well . . ." She paused dramatically. "There was the one . . . but I shouldn't mention it."

"I thought all Carole cared about was horses," Scott said.

"Yes," Stevie said. "Perhaps *that* was what was wrong with that dress."

"Huh?" Scott said.

"Well, it wasn't a dress exactly—just a sort of lace horse blanket."

"Hey, I didn't know she had a stamp collection. Has she got stamps from a lot of interesting countries?"

"She told me she has one from Canada," Stevie said. "And I think one from Kansas."

"Kansas is part of the U.S."

"I told her that," Stevie said. "Did Carole tell you about the contest she won last year?" Stevie had another bright idea.

"No," Scott said. "She doesn't talk too much about herself, you know."

"Well, she usually brags about this. I'm surprised."

"What kind of contest was it?" he asked.

"Frog jumping. Her little Mortimer went over thirty feet."

"Frog jumping?"

"Yeah, and a champion frog little Mort was, too."

"Was?" he asked dubiously.

"Until she had him stuffed. Keeps him on her bedside table. Gives all the live ones in her room something to live up to."

"She keeps frogs in her room?" he asked.

"Oh, yes. And she hasn't had a fly in there for years! The frogs eat 'em up as soon as they come through the window. There's a big future in frogs, you know."

"I thought Carole wanted to be a vet and work with horses."

"A lot of people make that mistake about her," Stevie said, groping to think of an explanation. "See, when she says vet, what she means is that she wants to be able to march in the Veterans Day parade. Wear one of those funny little hats, you know?"

"That's her life ambition?" Scott asked. Stevie liked the tone of his voice. It sounded like he was really getting worried. She was obviously succeeding in making Carole sound perfectly awful.

"Well, one of them," Stevie said. "Her other ambition is to learn to be a study-hall monitor. She always says it takes a certain kind of person to do that."

"It does," Scott agreed.

*Right*, Stevie said to herself. *It takes a real dweeb!* She was sure Scott was buying her story and that one of Carole's problems was about to be solved.

"Then, if she does well at that, maybe they'll let her have a whistle and a clipboard and she can be in charge of fire drills!"

"I had a friend once who was in charge of fire drills," Scott said.

"Really?" Stevie said.

"Well, he was supposed to be, but he was *so* stupid . . ."

"How stupid was he?" she asked automatically.

"He was so stupid that when the alarm went off he ran down to the home ec kitchen."

"Why'd he do that?" Stevie asked.

"So he could watch the rolls burn!"

"Huh? What are you talking about?"

"Not such a hot joke?" He paused, waiting for her to answer. She didn't know what to say. "Did you get that? *Hot* joke?"

Stevie looked at him quizzically. "Why are you telling me a joke?" she asked.

"Because you were telling *me* jokes," he said. "But I

think your routine is better than mine. Carole told me
you were very funny, and she's right."

Stevie couldn't believe it. She thought he had believed her! Well, maybe she had gone just a little bit
too far with the lace horse blanket.

"Listen," he said. "You work on that routine a bit
and you'll be on a stage very soon."

"Yeah, I know. The one leaving town, right?"

"That *was* the one I had in mind," he told her with
a grin. "There. That's the last bucket, isn't it? It's been
fun working with you this morning, Stevie. I'll probably stop by again tomorrow. I think it's time I tried my
hand at soaping tack."

As they stepped out of the final stall, Scott bowed to
Stevie graciously, and then turned and walked away.
After he had gone a few steps, he turned around to
wink at her.

Stevie put her hands back on her hips. "Well, I'll
be," she said.

"Be what?" Lisa asked from behind her. "Late for
class?"

"Not another comedian!" Stevie groaned. Lisa gave
her a weird look. Stevie shrugged. "I'll tell you later,"
she said. "Maybe."

CAROLE'S KITTEN, SNOWBALL, was very busy. Every time Carole moved the shoelace she was twiddling with, Snowball pounced.

"You're crazy, you know that, Snowball?" she asked. The kitten didn't pay any attention to her. In fact, he never paid any attention to anybody. He was the most contrary animal Carole had ever known. That was why she had named the coal-black kitten Snowball. Somehow, it just seemed to fit the little mischief-maker.

Carole heard a car in the driveway. It was midafternoon on Monday and she was home alone. Her father didn't usually get home until about five-thirty, but that was unmistakably the sound of their station wagon. She would recognize the noise of that faulty muffler anywhere!

She hobbled downstairs to greet her dad. Her ankle was a lot better, but it was still going to be a few days before she could get her boot on, much less ride. At least it was only a few days—not a few weeks, as Lynne had said. Carole curled her lip in distaste just thinking about the woman. She was still so upset about what had happened Saturday night that she had barely spoken to her father on Sunday. It was a rare thing when Carole didn't want to talk over something with her dad, but that was the case in this situation.

"Is something wrong, Dad?" she asked as he came in the door.

"Oh, no, honey, but things were slow at the office, so I signed out. I'd much rather be here with you. I want to be sure you're taking care of that foot."

"Oh, my foot's fine," she assured him.

"Well, I brought something for it anyway," he told her, showing her a special ice pack he had purchased. "This is an external pain-killer and here's something for *internal* application!" He held up a bag from TD's, the girls' favorite ice cream parlor at the shopping center.

"Hot fudge?" Carole asked.

"The very thing," he told her. "One for you. One for me. Now, sit down in the lounge chair and put your leg up on the footrest."

Smiling to herself, Carole did as she was told. Her father placed the new cool pack around her ankle gently and then he brought her a spoon and the sundae. He took the other sundae for himself and sat down on the sofa opposite her. They were quiet for a few moments while they opened their sundaes and had their first bites. Then the colonel looked his daughter square in the eye. "Okay, now I want you to tell me what the problem *really* is," he said. "You've been wandering around in a mopey state for a week and it got a lot worse on Saturday night. And I don't think it was because of your ankle."

"You mean I haven't fooled you?" she asked, toying with her spoon.

"Not a bit," he said. "And you haven't fooled anybody else, either. Scott called me at my office this morning to tell me that you were crying on Saturday *before* you hurt your ankle. Why don't you just tell me about it, honey? I hate to see you so unhappy—and I've got some wonderful news for you!"

Those were the words Carole had been dreading! She decided she might as well get it over with. "You first," she said, taking a deep breath. "Tell me your wonderful news." She couldn't bring herself to sound enthusiastic.

"You were sound asleep on Saturday, and holed up in your room yesterday, so I didn't have a chance to tell you that Lynne and I won the twist contest at the dance after you left. We were far and away the best."

"I knew you would," Carole said dully. "You're a great dancer. So where are you two going?"

"Us two?" the colonel responded, his face revealing his confusion.

"Yeah, you two won the contest, so you two will go someplace wonderful with the first prize, right?"

"Oh!" Colonel Hanson said. "No wonder . . ."

"No wonder what?" Carole asked.

"No wonder you've been so upset. You thought Lynne and I were going someplace and leaving you alone? Oh, honey, I'm sorry. This was all supposed to be a surprise, but surprises can backfire, I guess. No, the tickets were supposed to be for you and me. We were supposed to use them to go visit the Devines!"

"You and me, together, *alone*, at the dude ranch?" Carole asked, feeling a surge of hope. "But what about Lynne? What about your honeymoon?"

"*Honeymoon!* Oh, Carole!" The colonel shook his head with a rueful smile, then gave his daughter a fond look. "So *that* explains why you've been so upset. There's nothing really serious going on between Lynne and me, but I should have realized that you'd be wondering. But let me put your mind at ease. Carole, I'm not going to marry Lynne. She's nice enough, I guess, and she sure cares a lot, but she's the most bossy woman I've ever met! She's forever trying to change me."

"Me, too!" Carole said. She couldn't help grinning. So, her father thought Lynne was a pest, too!

"I mean, she's okay as a friend," Colonel Hanson continued. "And she's a good dancer. But I *don't* want to marry her." He came over to the chair and put his arms around his daughter. "If I ever do think about getting married again someday, you'll be the first one I talk to about it. After all, that would affect *your* life as much as mine. Your opinion would be very important in making a decision."

Carole gave her father a big hug. He *did* understand! She could see now that she had blown everything out of proportion.

"I'm glad you aren't going to marry Lynne. But shouldn't she get one of the tickets anyway, since she won the contest with you?" Carole asked.

"She probably should," he told her. "But she's scared to death of airplanes. Wouldn't think of traveling anyplace by plane. I'm afraid we're stuck with the tickets."

"Oh, wow!" Carole said, feeling comfortable for the first time in a long time. "So, when are we going to the dude ranch?"

"*That's* the bad news, Carole. My leave's been canceled because General Melendez has planned an inspection. So I just can't be away right now. And unfortunately, we have to use the tickets by a certain date, and I don't think I'll be free before then."

"Old General 'White Gloves' Melendez, you mean?" Carole said with a grin. She had always loved that nickname for the general who was famous for his tough inspections. Then she sighed. It would have been great to visit Kate with her father, but at least he wasn't getting married!

"The very one," her father said. "Anyway, I'm sorry to have to disappoint you, but we still have the tickets. Two of them. I thought that, considering how much fun you and your friends had with Kate when she was visiting, you might want to invite one of them to go along with you, using the second ticket. I wish I had three, but . . ."

"Oh, Dad! That would be fabulous! I can't believe it. I could actually go with one of my friends! But I can't stand to leave you."

"Stand it," he said reassuringly. "I'll be just fine. Besides, you know I'm no fun to be around when 'White Gloves' is on the base."

"You turn into an old grouch," she teased him.

"Maybe if I do, it'll be a way to convince Lynne that I'm not the man for her."

"Hey, that's a good idea. But how will I convince Scott I'm not the girl for him?" Carole asked.

"I didn't know we had the same problem," the colonel said.

"Neither did I," Carole said.

"What have you tried to solve it?" the colonel asked.

"I had him mucking out stables for an entire day. He loved it!"

"You should have seen Lynne on the obstacle course!"

"You took her on the o-course?" Carole asked, astonished. Quantico was famous for its rough physical training. It was hard to imagine Lynne swarming up a twenty-five foot rope.

"She told me it was better than her health club!"

"We should get these two together," Carole said. "Lynne and Scott would make quite a pair."

"That's true, but I don't think it will solve our problem. In fact, it could compound it."

Carole was thinking about what her father had said when the phone rang.

"I'll get it," she said.

"I thought your ankle still hurt," the colonel said in surprise.

"Not when the phone's ringing," she told him, springing to her feet.

In fact, her ankle was feeling a lot better. And the rest of her was feeling better, too. She reached for the phone. It was Stevie.

At the sound of Stevie's voice, Carole recalled that she still had a few little problems to solve. One of them was going to be deciding which one of her friends she would invite to the dude ranch. That was a problem she wasn't ready to solve yet. On the spot, she decided not to mention it to Stevie.

Stevie didn't notice her hesitation. She was talking too much and too fast to be aware of Carole's uncertainty.

". . . And Scott carried one zillion water buckets for me. I thought maybe I could help you by telling him all the things about you that aren't so nice—"

"Like what?" Carole demanded.

"Oh, well, you know, like how you make your own clothes and you want to be a study-hall monitor and march in the Veterans Day parade. Well, that sort of thing."

"Stevie! Those things aren't true!"

"I know. I was just trying to help," she said.

"By making me sound like a nerd?"

"Don't worry, Carole. He didn't believe a word of it anyway. If you want, though, I can try again tomorrow. He's coming to clean tack with me."

"Thanks, but no thanks! This guy is too much," Carole said after a moment.

"He's really kind of nice, you know."

"Sure he is. He's almost too nice. There's really nothing wrong with him at all, except that I don't want to go out with him. Maybe be his friend, sure. I'm just not ready for dates."

"Did you tell him that?" Stevie asked.

"No, of course not," Carole said. "The whole idea has been to turn him off."

"And the whole idea's been totally unsuccessful," Stevie reminded her.

"That's for sure. It's not working for either me or Dad," Carole told her.

"Your dad? What's this about?"

Quickly, Carole filled Stevie in on the *real* story of the romance between Lynne and the colonel.

"I can't believe it. You guys are in the same boat," Stevie said.

"And it's sinking, fast!" Carole concluded.

Stevie laughed. "It may not be as bad as you think. For one thing, you got some lousy advice."

"From *you!*" Carole said.

"That was the first time around. This time, I think you should try the direct method instead of the indirect one. After all, Scott and Lynne aren't mind readers! Say," she said, changing the subject. "Are you coming to Pine Hollow tomorrow? We want to have a Saddle Club meeting at TD's after class. Are you going to be there?"

"You bet I am!" Carole said. "If I'm not there, you'll

have Scott scrubbing every bit of tack in the place and believing that it's my lifelong ambition to drive a tractor-trailer!"

"I never thought of that!" Stevie teased.

"So don't start now!" Carole teased back. "Anyway, I don't know if I'll be able to ride, but I'll be at the stables. See you tomorrow."

"Bye-bye," Stevie said, and then hung up the phone.

When Carole hung up, she returned to the living room. "It was Stevie," she said to her father. "And she had the most amazing suggestion. Listen to this wild and crazy idea of hers," Carole began.

"YOU REALLY WANT to soap saddles?" Carole asked Scott when he appeared at Pine Hollow the next morning at chore time.

"Whatever," he said agreeably. "I just like being with you," he added.

"Well, I like being with you," she told him, handing him a can of saddle soap and demonstrating the short circular motions that cleaned the leather. "And I think we could be good friends." She applied some polish to her own saddle and worked at it for a few seconds. Scott was working silently, waiting for her to go on. "In fact, I'd like to be your *good* friend," she concluded.

"And not my *girl*friend?" he asked, getting the message.

"Yes," she told him. "I'd rather be your friend than your girlfriend. Of course, Max'll be furious with me if that means you won't be doing chores here anymore!" she teased.

Scott laughed. "No, it's no problem. I'm only going to be here with my folks for another couple of days anyway. But I'll do chores until then. I like working around horses. I think I'll do more of it when I get home to Ohio."

"So you really got to like horses this vacation, then?" Carole asked.

"You bet," he told her. "It's been a great vacation. I've gotten a love of horses. But best of all, I've got a new friend."

Carole looked up at him from her saddle. He was smiling warmly at her. He understood. Things could be pretty easy when you tried to do them the direct way, not the roundabout way. She grinned back at Scott.

"Will you write to me?" Scott asked.

"Sure I will, if you'll write and tell me about the horses you work with in Ohio."

"It's a deal," he said. They shook saddle-soapy hands.

"IT WAS YOUR wild and crazy idea, Stevie," Carole said to her friend that afternoon at TD's. "You told me that

I should just be direct. So I told that to Dad. He'd been doing the same thing I had. He even had Lynne out on the obstacle course at the base—and she loved it as much as Scott loved mucking out stalls! Anyway, he called her last night and explained how he felt. He told me she seemed almost relieved! It worked so well for him that I tried it this morning. Guess what?"

"You broke his heart?" Lisa asked.

"Nope. We're going to be friends. He's a really nice guy, you know. I think we may even be good friends! Who knows, maybe one day I'll even visit him in Ohio!"

Stevie and Lisa were very excited about their news for Carole and they were about to get down to business when the waitress arrived to take their orders. Stevie ordered a blueberry sundae on coffee ice cream. She always tried to be outrageous. Lisa accused her of eating weird combinations to keep from having to share with her friends. Stevie denied it, but she never had to share, either! Lisa ordered a butterscotch sundae. "On vanilla ice cream," she said pointedly to the waitress, who seemed a bit relieved after Stevie's order. Carole asked for a root-beer float.

"It's our turn to tell, now," Stevie said, looking at Lisa, who nodded agreement.

"Tell what?" Carole asked. "Have you two been keeping a secret?"

"It wasn't supposed to be a secret, but once it started happening and it didn't happen to you, it just sort of turned into a secret. At first it was a good secret, but then it became a bad secret, and now it's just a funny secret," Lisa explained.

"What *is* she talking about?" Carole asked Stevie, laughing at Lisa's jumbled sentence.

"Our attempt at being models," Stevie said, twirling her hair around her fingers casually.

"Models! You two! Tell me!" Carole said excitedly.

Then, because they had been holding it all in for so long, the whole story about their ill-fated careers as models came tumbling out. Stevie told about the class Carole had missed where Jackie was photographing everybody, and then Lisa told Carole about the phone call.

"Really, the most fun part of this whole thing was our daydreams," Lisa said. "I don't know about yours, Stevie, but mine were terrific."

"Mine were in Paris," Stevie said airily.

"Mine were in a sports car in Monte Carlo!" Lisa announced.

"It sounds like the dream life of a model isn't the same as the *actual* life of a model. Is that true?" Carole asked.

Her best friends nodded. "We're sadder, but wiser," Stevie said. "In fact, it was awful." Then they told Carole, in gruesome detail, just how much fun it was groveling in the dirt to keep a saddle from tipping, or holding onto a horse's halter for what seemed like hours so that the nameplate on the halter wouldn't gleam too brightly in the sun.

"And the worst part was that there aren't even any photographs of us! Just a little bit of my knee in *one* picture."

"You're being too modest," Lisa said. "Remember that Jackie said she thought it was a particularly good knee."

"Give me a break!" Stevie groaned.

"Well, look at it this way," Carole said brightly. "A lot of girls dream of being models for years and are really disappointed when their dreams don't come true. You two already know better, don't you? That's got to be worth something."

"Trust her to find the bright side of that experience," Stevie joked. "Now that *her* problems have been solved." Carole laughed.

"Actually, there is a bright side," Lisa said. "We got paid for our work. We each got fifty dollars!"

"Not bad," Carole said. "What are you going to do with it?"

Lisa and Stevie exchanged glances. Then Stevie nudged Lisa. Carole couldn't understand why both of her friends seemed a little embarrassed. "Ahem," Stevie said, looking at Lisa again.

Lisa nodded and spoke. "We both felt pretty bad that you weren't included in the modeling job, even when it turned out that it wasn't much fun. Although it would have been more fun with the three of us together. Anyway, in order to make it up to you that you didn't get to model, we've decided to give you all the money we earned. If you add that to the money you've already saved up to visit Kate's dude ranch, you *should* have enought for the round-trip airfare now. So"—she reached into her pocket and brought out an envelope with Carole's name on it—"here it is. For you. From us."

Carole could barely believe her ears. Her friends were not only making an incredible and wonderful sacrifice for her, they were solving an awful problem she had. She *still* hadn't decided which one she should invite to go with her—and now she didn't have to decide at all.

"This is incredible!" Carole said.

"Well, generous, yes, but incredible, definitely not," Stevie said matter-of-factly.

"No, I mean the coincidence."

"What does coincidence have to do with it?" Lisa asked.

"It has to do with my father's dancing," Carole said.

Stevie scrunched her eyebrows and looked over at

Lisa. "Give her a few bucks and she goes crazy," she announced.

"No, I haven't," Carole said, giggling. "But remember how Lisa just said that everything is more fun when we're together? Well, going to the dude ranch will be more fun if all three of us go together, too!" Then, while her friends listened excitedly, she told them about the tickets her father had won and how they could use them.

"Hey, this'll be great!" Lisa said. "I just can't believe it!"

"I can," Stevie quipped. All three girls laughed together.

"Here's to The Saddle Club's first western field trip," Stevie added as the waitress brought their order to the table. She lifted a spoonful of blueberries. "It'll be outstanding," she pronounced.

"Hear, hear," Lisa said, giggling.

"It'll be *absolutely* wonderful," Carole told them.

And as the three friends lifted their spoons and clicked them together, they all knew Carole was right. Everything The Saddle Club did together was wonderful—well, *almost* everything!

## ABOUT THE AUTHOR

BONNIE BRYANT is the author of more than twenty books for young readers, including the best-selling novelizations of *The Karate Kid* movies. The Saddle Club books are her first for Bantam Books. She wrote her first book six years ago and has been busy at her word processor ever since. (For her first three years as an author, Ms. Bryant was also working in the office of a publishing company. In 1986, she left her job to write full-time.)

Whenever she can, Ms. Bryant goes horseback riding in her hometown, New York City. She's had many riding experiences in the city's Central Park that have found their way into her Saddle Club books—and lots which haven't!

The author and her two sons live together in an apartment in Greenwich Village that is just too small for a horse.

YOUR PONY

A Young Person's Guide to Buying,
Keeping and Riding Ponies

Michael and Marilyn Clayton

Do you know how to look after a pony properly? Where
to keep it, and how to feed it? How to jump a
combination fence – or how to ride safely on the roads?

All the answers to all your questions about owning and
riding a pony can be found in this invaluable guide
that's full of sound advice and practical information on
how to get the very best out of owning a pony – from
choosing your first ever pony, to learning how to
canter, gallop and jump, and all the fun you and your
pony can have taking part in competitions.

Fully illustrated with photographs and line drawings.

SBN 1852 251263
£12.99 hardback

PARTRIDGE PRESS

**SWEET VALLEY TWINS**

Follow the adventures of Jessica, Elizabeth and all their
friends at Sweet Valley as twelve-year-olds. A super series
with one new title every month!

SWEET VALLEY TWINS SUPER CHILLERS

SWEET VALLEY TWINS SUPER EDITIONS

We hope you enjoyed reading this book. If you would like to receive further information about available titles in the Bantam series, just write to the address below, with your name and address: Kim Prior, Bantam Books, 61–63 Uxbridge Road, Ealing, London W5 5SA.

If you live in Australia or New Zealand and would like more information about the series, please write to:

Sally Porter
Transworld Publishers
(Australia) Pty Ltd
15–25 Helles Avenue
Moorebank
NSW 2170
AUSTRALIA

Kiri Martin
Transworld Publishers (NZ) Ltd
3 William Pickering Drive
Albany
Auckland
NEW ZEALAND

All Bantam and Young Adult books are available at your bookshop or newsagent, or can be ordered from the following address: Corgi/Bantam Books, Cash Sales Department, PO Box 11, Falmouth, Cornwall, TR10 9EN.

Please list the title(s) you would like, and send together with a cheque or postal order to cover the cost of the book(s) plus postage and packing charges of £1.00 for one book, £1.50 for two books, and an additional 30p for each subsequent book ordered to a maximum of £3.00 for seven or more books.

**(The above applies only to readers in the UK, and BFPO)**

Overseas customers (including Eire), please allow £2.00 for postage and packing for the first book, an additional £1.00 for a second book, and 50p for each subsequent title ordered.